TENDER
EVE AINSWORTH

SCHOLASTIC

Scholastic Children's Books
An imprint of Scholastic Ltd
Euston House, 24 Eversholt Street, London, NW1 1DB, UK
Registered office: Westfield Road, Southam, Warwickshire, CV47 0RA
SCHOLASTIC and associated logos are trademarks and/or
registered trademarks of Scholastic Inc.

First published in the UK by Scholastic Ltd, 2018

Text copyright © Eve Ainsworth, 2018

The right of Eve Ainsworth to be identified as the author
of this work has been asserted by her.

ISBN 978 1407 16430 4

A CIP catalogue record for this book
is available from the British Library.

Printed by CPI Group (UK) Ltd, Croydon, CR0 4YY

Papers used by Scholastic Children's Books are made
from wood grown in sustainable forests.

1 3 5 7 9 10 8 6 4 2

www.scholastic.co.uk

For Noah.
The bravest boy I know.

MARTY

Some people struggle to get out of bed in the morning. People like my mum. They say it's the worst time of their day. For them, it's like the moment of waking is the moment when everything becomes too much. They can't physically move; they feel like lead. They can't get out of bed; they don't want to face another day. They just want to sleep.

But I don't get that. I don't get that at all.

It's the *going* to bed that I can't stand — the laying down on the mattress and staring up at the ceiling, night after night. Watching the darkness. *That's* what gets to me, because *that's* when the thinking really starts. And when it starts,

I can't make it stop.

Give me the mornings anytime. Give me the light.

Please take away the dark.

Mum hadn't got out of bed for four days straight, which was some kind of tragic record. I guess just being "up" became too much for her. She needed to rest again. Needed to shut herself away. Her door was slightly open, and if I listened carefully I could hear her breathing. Nothing else. If I went into her room, she would lie there perfectly still. Sometimes she would talk, but her words always sounded wooden and flat. This morning she had asked for a cup of tea and some toast. That was a slight improvement. At least she was eating.

I was cooking when they came. OK, "cooking" was probably stretching the term a little – but baked beans *are* a type of food and they needed cooking, so I guess it counts. And we had food this time. At least I wasn't eating dry cereal out of the mixing bowl again. I had to try and get Mum to eat something – even if it was just a bit of toast. Anyway, I was heating the beans when the hammering on the door began: short, sharp raps on the glass that seemed to shake the entire flat. They couldn't ring the doorbell – *that* broke ages ago. I was a bit worried, because that glass isn't the strongest and they were banging pretty hard. The beans bubbled in front of me, the orange sauce thickening and staining the sides of the pan. I moved the wooden spoon slowly, crushing them. I had an idea who it was. I guess deep down I'd been expecting them. I'd just always hoped they'd find something more important to do with their time. Reaching for my phone, I punched out a message to J.

Trouble – get home now.

Of course J was out. Just nipped to the pub, he said. Just gone for a quick one. I couldn't blame him. Why should he have to babysit me all the time? I'm hardly his responsibility.

Another rap, harder now.

My stomach lurched. Should I wake Mum or

leave her be? What was the best thing to do?

Probably neither.

"OK, OK!" I said under my breath.

I moved the pan and switched off the gas. I removed the almost-too-dry-to-be-edible bread from the toaster. I walked down our thin, dark corridor and opened the door to their fake, all-knowing faces. Two women smiled at me. One was tall with bright red hair and matching lipstick, the other shorter with a mess of blonde curls piled on her head. Their lips seemed to be pressed into matching grins.

The taller woman leant towards me slightly. "Martin? Martin Field?"

"Marty," I replied. "It's just Marty."

I could tell her that I was named after a character in Mum's favourite film. I could tell her that Mum watched *Back to the Future* at least once a week and that because of this I knew all the lines off by heart. I could tell her all these things, but it would be pointless – they thought they knew us already.

"I'm sorry." Her grin widened. "Is your mum in?

Or your stepdad ... John?"

John? I imagined calling J by that name, but no way did it suit him. He'd laugh in my face.

"J? He's not my stepdad. He's my mum's boyfriend and he's on his way home now."

I hope.

"And he's your legal guardian."

"Yes."

At the moment, anyway.

I wondered if this was my opportunity to tell them to go away, to come back another time, to leave us all in peace – but then I heard the crash of the lift doors further down the deck. Damn, it was too late. He was back.

J half-jogged towards us, his lanky body moving awkwardly, his long, dark hair swinging in front of his face. He pushed the sides away with his hands and coughed his guts up loudly. For a skinny guy he was dead unfit.

"Sorry, sorry. I was held up. Was seeing a bloke about potential work." He turned to me and smirked.

Work. Yeah, right.

J's "work" involved odd building jobs here and there. Most of the time he was down the pub or the betting shop, spunking his wages against the wall.

"It's fine. You're here now." The tall lady smiled back towards me. "I'm Jenny, we met before at your school? This is my trainee, Debbie."

I stared back at her. Did she seriously think I would forget? The one time I actually go school and two social workers show up and pull me into a meeting room. They tell you they just want to "chat", that they have "concerns and worries". But it's all crap. They just want to cause trouble. Stick their noses in where it's not wanted. I told them not to come here. I told them not to bother, but I knew they wouldn't listen.

The blonde girl smiled at us nervously. I frowned back. I'm not sure why. All this niceness was doing my head in. Why weren't they saying what they were really thinking? They didn't like us. Not really. You could just tell. You could see them judging us, their eyes drifting down to my clothes: old tracksuit bottoms, a manky top and holey socks.

"I was making dinner," I said. "We haven't eaten yet."

"We won't keep you long," Jenny said lightly, shifting a large-looking folder from one hip to the other. "I just need to discuss a few things with you both. Make a few arrangements. There are certain things we need to put in place before—"

"Jo has been a bit poorly," J said quickly. "She's resting in bed at the moment. We've been looking after her."

Jenny nodded. "Yes, so Marty said. I only want a quick word. It honestly won't take long."

I hated having them inside the flat. That was the worst. They could see the total mess of our lives – the wet clothes on the radiators, last night's cups still on the floor, my box of latest finds stuffed in the corner, the Xbox controllers dumped on the chair where we'd been playing until late last night. I'd actually tidied up a bit. Picked up J's beer cans. Thrown away the pizza boxes. It still stunk like musty socks in here though. It was a thick smell that stuck to the side of your throat, making you want to cough. I only really noticed it when I stepped back in. It was chaos. *Our* chaos. I didn't mind it, but I knew other people would.

Obviously things were better when Mum was well, but when she got ill things drifted a bit. It was always that way. But we'd get on top of it again. We always did, that was just how it worked here. Jenny and Debbie perched on the edge of the sofa. It was comical really – they looked like they might fall off any minute. J edged out and went to the bedroom. I heard him talking softly to Mum and her louder protests filtered back. She didn't want to get up. She would, though. She had to.

"We don't have fleas," I said, staring at them both, daring them to sit on our chairs properly.

I saw Debbie's eyes scan the old cushions like she didn't quite believe me. One arm stroked the other arm.

"No – no, of course not," she said. But she didn't move any further back.

J walked back into the room, laughing.

"It's a bit of a mess in here, but what do you expect, two lads together? I've been busy and Marty is at school. We just need Jo back on her feet. She loves to clean, does our Jo."

"I'm not here to judge you," Jenny said sweetly. "But how long exactly has Jo been ill?"

I saw J hesitate, his face stiffened. "Not long. She just has a bug, that's all. Nothing odd about that."

"I didn't say there was. I was just concerned, that's all."

Liar.

We heard the shuffling first and then the soft cough. Mum slipped into the room, her clothing rustling as she moved. She looked awful, a dressing gown pulled tight around her thin body and her thick, messy hair pulled back into a loose ponytail. It was like she hadn't slept for weeks.

"Why are you here? I don't need this," she said, her voice raspy and accusing. "I just need rest. Peace. I don't need the likes of you coming to my flat."

"Did you get my phone messages, Jo? Do you know who we are?"

"My phone is turned off. Like I said, I need to *rest*."

Mum perched on the arm of the sofa and started to rub the skin on her arm.

"But yeah, I know who are. Bloody social – you have it written all over you. What's all this about? We don't need any help. I didn't ask for this."

Jenny rifled through her papers, sighed a little, and then eased herself back into our chair, thoughts of fleas obviously forgotten. "We've had ... calls. Anonymous, but people have reported shouting from this property. Arguing. They said you sounded distressed..."

Mum shrugged. "I was probably arguing with J. We have a fiery relationship, that's all."

"But we get on fine, don't we, babe!" J said, too loudly.

Calm down, mate. If you keep grinning like that, they're bound to think you're covering something up.

"... and we've had concerns from Marty's school. His behaviour, and..."

And let the interfering begin.

"He's doing well at school. He's always going on about it!" Mum said, her eyes flashing at me.

Jenny looked between Mum and me. "You think Marty has been going to school?"

She started to rifle through her file and drew out a sheet of paper after spending some time peering at the words written on it. I could feel the tension burning through my body. I wanted to pace the room. No, screw that, I wanted to *leave* the room.

"You haven't been going to school, have you, Marty?" she said finally, looking at me. Not so much a question as a statement.

I didn't answer.

J moved in front of me, with a face full of fake shock and disgust. "What? Where have you been, then?"

He was so rubbish at lying.

I shrugged. "There's no point being there."

"Marty, your attendance is currently at 62%. This is far below where it should be. We need to see improvement. You are a bright and able student. You could do really well."

I stared at her. What did she know?

"You need to sort it out," Mum said, not very

convincingly. She half laughed. "You don't want to end up like me, now, do you?"

She had a point there.

"I hate school," I told them. "It's a waste of time."

"Do you think your mum needs to hear that, Marty? If she's not well at the moment, she doesn't need to worry about you, too. She needs to see that you're OK. She also doesn't need to be worrying about you truanting – you know she could be fined for this."

Fined? Like the school would bother. They were probably glad to see the back of me.

"Don't tell me what my mum needs," I said. "I *know* what my mum needs."

"And what *is* that?" Jenny was peering right up at me, eyes wide now. "What *does* she need?"

"Me. That's all. We don't need you lot poking your noses in." I could feel myself getting angry. "I'm not a loser, you know. I have plans. Mum knows them. She believes in me. She thinks I could do really well if I put my mind to it."

Jenny sighed and pushed her sheet of paper back into the folder. "I get that. I really do. But we're not your enemy, Marty. We are here to help. *All of you*. We understand that things must be hard, especially after your dad's death."

I went back to staring. I was getting seriously fed up now.

Do not go there... Just don't.

J snorted. "You wanna help? Find me a decent job."

"I want you to let us help you," Jenny said, still looking straight at me.

I shook my head. "I don't need help from anyone."

Later, in my room, I sat holding a stupid leaflet and lousy card with Jenny's contact details on it. I don't know why I didn't just rip in up in front of their faces. In the other room, they were still talking to Mum. I wanted them to leave her alone. She was tired. She didn't need the extra stress.

J stood in the doorway, leaning lazily against the door frame. He was smoking, which was taking the piss. Mum would hate that, but I didn't have the energy to stop him.

"You have to go," he said. "It's the only way to

get them off our cases."

"What, back to school?" My stomach lurched. "No way."

"She's right. Your mum needs it calm here. We just need to do our best to keep things ... well, normal." He took a long drag and puffed out smoke into my room. "And to be honest, mate, I don't want those women hanging around here poking their noses in. You know I'm doing cash-in-hand work at the moment. They might try to cut my benefit."

"So it's all about *you*..."

"Not at all! But if I'm earning less, it affects us all, don't it? Think about it — we don't need that interference, that's all. People prying where they're not wanted."

I sighed. "Whatever."

"Good lad."

"And this?" I waved the leaflet in his face. "This will help her *how*, exactly?"

J shrugged. "Nah. That's to help you, mate."

I stared down at the large writing, the soppy faces grinning up at me.

YOUNG CARERS
MEET, CHAT, CHILL

"Seriously?"

"Just go to one meeting. See what's it like. Make them think you're cool about it."

What, sitting around with a bunch of sad losers moaning about their lives? Watching them wring their hands and open up about their problems? I'd rather spew my guts in front of them. But the thought of months with the social sniffing around us made my blood run cold.

I shook my head. "Tell them to stick it," I said.

I turned away from him then but I heard his sigh as he left the room.

Such a loser.

But in a weird way I still liked having him round. He was better than nothing and he stopped me being alone with Mum. But there was no way I was going to some crap like this.

I could deal with everything my way.

I always did.

DAISY

The room was set up perfectly. The throw was draped over the sofa and the cushions arranged all around us so we'd be super cosy. The lights were turned down low and the curtains drawn. The table was stacked with sweets, crisps and a great big bowl of popcorn. In the corner the baby monitor flickered.

"Mum, this is amazing," I said.

She smiled. "You think? Did I get enough in? I've got a pizza for later if you're still hungry."

Dad had gone out earlier for his monthly "lads' night", so this was our time – just her and me. I always looked forward to it. It was time we so rarely had now.

"What are we watching, anyway?"

"It's up to you." Mum hovered the remote over Netflix. "There's bound to be something on here – or we could watch an old favourite?"

"A *favourite?*" I giggled, helping myself to handful of popcorn. "You mean another Adam Sandler movie..."

"What?" Mum looked at me in fake shock. "I don't know what you mean... He's a great actor."

"You're totally in love with him, that's what."

"I'm not!" Her cheeks had reddened but her grin was spreading. She looked so young when she smiled. "He just makes me laugh, that's all. I mean – I guess he is handsome in a quirky sort of way. I do like unusual men."

I snuggled up next to her. "*I know.*"

My dad was pretty quirky. Mohican haircut, tattoos and piercings in his ears. When the two of them were younger they looked so cool. I've seen the photos – Mum with her short blonde hair and Dad towering over her in his motorbike leathers. It's weird that I look nothing like them. I was the plump, red-haired daughter with glasses. I looked like I belonged to a completely different family.

"This is nice," I said, leaning against Mum's tiny body, breathing in her soft sweet scent.

"It is." She stroked my hair. "How's Martha? Have you two made up?"

"Yeah, it's all cool."

"Is she still in love with that kid in your year?"

"Martha is *always* in love with some loser," I sighed. "But school is dull, as always."

"And you're OK?"

I felt a little tug inside me. That need to talk, to empty out some of the heaviness I was carrying. I buried myself deeper into the side of her body and sighed. "Actually, Mum, there is something. I—"

I felt Mum stiffen, and she sat up, knocking me back a little. Her eyes were no longer on the TV; instead, she was staring at the baby monitor, looking for the small beads of blue light that flickered up and down.

The lights had stopped moving.

Mum jumped up.

"I'm sorry, Daisy," she said. "I need to check on Harry."

I turned back to the TV and started watching the film alone.

I held his hand the first time he died.

He had just been a tiny baby, with hands like seashells – so pink they were almost see-through. He hadn't been with us for long – born a month early and kept in hospital because of his size. It was my first visit when it all went horribly wrong. Suddenly the noises he was making in my arms weren't right and I remember my mum shouting something frantic at the nurse in the corner of the room.

I've never told anyone this, but I knew. I knew something had changed in the way he felt in my arms. There was a shift in weight and his eyes no longer focused on me.

The nurse snatched him from my arms and I remember my mum crying out, shouting words that made no sense.

"Be careful... He's so small... She only had him for a minute... She didn't do anything!"

I said nothing but I felt everything, because I

thought that the first time I'd ever held my baby brother, I'd ended up hurting him. Of course, later I found out it wasn't like that at all.

Harry *had* technically died, but the doctors at St Andrews had saved him. And yes, it had happened the first time I'd held him, but it was nothing to do with me. I was just the nine-year-old girl caught up in the middle of it all. Mum said she always knew Harry was poorly – that she knew when he was growing inside her tummy. She said she would talk to him, stroking her tummy extra hard like she was willing him to be all right. Nothing had been picked up in tests, so this was just her instinct – a feeling she had carried for a long time. And when he was born, Mum had had a look of concern permanently on her face. Dad told me she was tired. He was pretty calm about it all. Harry had been born a little early and he was smaller than other babies. Mum was bound to feel protective. And we all assumed things would get better. That Harry would grow stronger, that Mum would relax.

We were wrong.

Things would get so much worse than we'd imagined.

That first time Harry's heart stopped beating, it was like a part of mine froze too. Sounds crazy, but I swear it's true. Even now, every time I look at him I feel that panic. I'm always worrying it's going to happen again. Always waiting for the next time his body lets him down. For ages, I didn't really know what was going on with my brother. I just knew that he was ill. I had imagined that I'd have a baby at home, cooing in his cot. My parents would be there and everything would be normal and safe. Instead, I ended up practically living with Nan while my parents went back and forth to the hospital. Whenever I saw them, they looked different. Usually quiet, always stressed. They talked in low voices so I couldn't hear, and their eyes never made contact with mine. I suddenly felt detached, like I wasn't part of their world.

All I was told was that Harry had trouble breathing. He kept catching infections and no one knew why, but there were "concerns about his blood". The last part worried me the most. His blood? What could be wrong with his blood? My heart ached when I imagined them taking blood from his little arms, his tiny legs. I think my mum might've felt that as well, because she seemed to be shrinking in front of me, getting paler, thinner, smaller. It was like they were draining her too. After months of drifting in this weird existence, my mum sat me down.

"We think we know what Harry has," she said, her words shuddering. "We know what's wrong."

I looked at her face, soft and pretty. I could almost trace the lines where her tears had fallen. Her eyes were permanently red these days.

"Harry has muscular dystrophy. The doctors think he has a particular type called Duchenne."

"What is that? Will he get better?"

She took a breath. I could see her tongue working in her mouth like she was actually finding the right words to say.

"No. It's progressive, Daisy. That means his muscles will get weaker and weaker. He'll probably need a wheelchair a little later and medication to help his heart. His heart is a muscle too, of course ... so that will also get weaker with time."

"I don't understand."

"Neither do I. Not yet, anyway." Mum's voice was shaking. "Try to think of his muscles like a stained-glass window in an old church. The stained glass has black frames around it, to protect it, to keep it in place, and muscles are the same. They need something to keep them in place and to stop them from rubbing and wearing away."

"And Harry's muscles are different...?"

"Harry's muscles are like stained glass with no support at all. He's very, very fragile."

"Will he...?" I thought of that time again. Of holding his tiny body. Of knowing that he stopped breathing in my arms.

Oh my God ... that would happen again. My brother *would* die again.

I realized my mum was holding my hand, gripping it tightly. Tears were flowing fast down her face.

"We just have to make his life as wonderful as

possible," she said. "We've been told to love him as much as we can and make every day count."

I didn't realize until she pulled me towards her that I was crying too.

The baby monitor flickered again and I could hear the soft murmur of Harry's voice, followed by a small cough. Quite often he stopped breathing at night and he managed to wake himself up, but Mum couldn't be sure so she needed to check. How much sleep did she get – did she spend all her time just watching and waiting? Worrying that this would be the night when his body would forget to breathe again? It was like he was still a baby. He wasn't of course – he was five now. But he was still as vulnerable as a newborn.

She came downstairs. Her eyes were redder and her lips were drawn into a tight line.

"He's a little wheezy," she said. "He's caught another cold, probably from school. There's just too many bugs going around at the moment."

"Do you want me to call Dad?"

"No, not yet. Let him enjoy his night in peace."

She sat down and picked up the monitor, cradling it in her hands. "It'll be OK," she said. "I'll just keep an eye on it. We can still watch something."

I put the TV back on and tried to nestle back into Mum's now stiff and solid body. She didn't even notice what the film was until about twenty minutes in. Her eyes were fixed on the blue lights of the monitor. And from then on, so were mine.

MARTY

Mum was back in bed. This time with the door closed.

"I'll get her some flowers on the way back," J said. "That'll make her feel better. Show her we care."

I stared at him, wondering if he was for real. My belly growled and I wasn't quite sure if it was hunger or the anticipation of what was to come. It was strange, that feeling – knowing that I really wanted Mum to be better, that I wanted her up and about again, but also knowing that that could cause problems of its own.

"You *are* going to school, yeah?" he said, poking my bag with his dirty finger. "I mean, you told the social you would – so it's best to make an effort, right? They'll be checking. They'll be coming back next week."

"I'm going. I told you."

I walked to the fridge and opened it. "We need some food. If we cooked something nice for Mum it might help."

"Yeah, I'll sort it."

"Not just chips. She'll go crazy."

"I said *I'll sort it*," J said, a little louder. "I'm owed some money. I'll pick up some bits later."

"And in the meantime I'll eat . . . what? Ketchup?"

He sighed. "Do you ever stop *whinging?* Here. . ." He dug around in his pocket. "Here's a couple of quid, get something on your way in."

"Cheers, J."

He looked up at me. His eyes were shiny bright, his hair slicked back into a ponytail. "See? We look after other, don't we? Everything's going to be all right. It's all going to be perfect now."

I walked out the room feeling sick. As I passed Mum's bedroom, I thought of her lying in bed staring at the ceiling. What did she think about in there, day in, day out? Maybe she wasn't actually thinking at all — maybe she was like a computer when it crashed, a blue screen waiting to be restarted. I felt like I could puke in the doorway.

How the hell was everything gonna be perfect? How could it *ever* be?

I walked as slowly as I could to St David's. It's really not a place you rush to, school — not unless you're a complete loon. On the way I ducked into the local newsagent and bought an energy drink, which I figured would keep me going until lunch. They also had some cheap chocolate bars on offer, a bit rank because they were so close to their sell-by date, but I couldn't stress about that. I grabbed one, feeling a stab of guilt as I walked past the shelves of tinned Roses and Quality Street — Mum's favourites.

Another day. Another day I would treat her.

It was a gloomy, misty-rainy type of day. My jacket was heavy and thick but seemed to soak up the wet and soon started to cling to me. It had a musty smell that was only getting worse — I swear, my clothes never smelt good, probably because they could never dry properly in our stupid, damp flat.

Who can afford to keep the heating on all day? And I knew my uniform was getting too small, but what was the point of buying new stuff when I would be leaving the old place soon?

For a moment my mind flicked to Dad. He got away, obviously. But not in a good way. She hasn't been the same since he left us behind, and it's been over three years since he died. If Dad were still alive we would be all right. We could make it work. But now it was just down to me.

I stuffed the chocolate into my mouth too quickly, then paused to wash it all down with the syrupy orange fizz. I saw a group of Greenfield girls out of the corner of my eye. They seemed to move in a purple rush of giggles and shouts. These were the clever kids, the Greenfield elite. I had been one of them, once – a fact that seems laughable now. One tall blonde girl looked over at me and caught me staring.

"Oy! Davey-boy – what you gawping at?"

They all giggled even more.

"Sort your trousers out, Davey-boy!" another one shrieked and they erupted into laughter.

I looked down at the material flapping just above my ankles. Why should I care about a skanky uniform? It said nothing about me, nothing at all. Stupid idiots judging me – just because they had perfect lives. What gave them the right to look at me like that?

I flicked them the finger and let the usual curses escape my mouth. I knew my face had turned ugly – it was twisting with every word – but I couldn't care less. And anyway, shouting at them felt better.

"Bloody nutter," one of them muttered, and I shot them a filthy look as they scuttled away.

I guess it could be worse. I see other kids walk in, getting grief all the time. Like that year seven, Lucas David, with the greasy hair. He gets beaten up most mornings just for looking different. At least I don't get that. At least I'm not another playground victim. I just get ignored. I'm the one they avoid.

I'm the headcase.

It wasn't always that way – I used to do all right. I was at Greenfield's then, living in a totally different world. I played football with lads like Archie and Kwaime and got picked first for games. Back then, stuff wasn't as bad. Mum had a job, Dad was still alive, we had money coming in. I even kind of liked school, which seems crazy now. But then things started to change. I guess I did too.

I never meant for that thing to happen to Kwaime. *Never.* But no one will ever understand that. They still talk about it now – even here. I see the looks.

So now I walk alone in a school where I'll never belong. And it's better to pretend everything is OK. But of course it isn't. On the street is one thing, but at school it's much worse. And I always try and kid myself that this is no big deal. That school is just a stepping stone to something else. Something better. And so, really, none of this matters, because one day I can leave it all behind.

But, seriously. Who am I kidding?

I ended up just watching again. I never *plan* to bunk school, it's just it feels wrong when I actually get there. The sick feeling of dread comes back and I have to force myself to walk. I usually end up rooted to the spot, like a pathetic statue looking in through the chain-link fence.

I watched the lads playing football on the AstroTurf and wondered what they'd do if I went over and joined in. Tell me where to go, probably. Maybe just walk off. Nothing *too* bad, though – they wouldn't dare. Over by the door I could see my head of year, Mr Terry, chatting to a sixth-former and laughing. I like him – he's one of the few teachers who seem to actually listen. I could've wandered over and talked to him. Told him I was back. But I didn't move. The football game was ending, the bell was ringing, everyone was going inside and I was frozen to the spot.

Then I found myself moving again, but in the opposite direction.

The market was packed, as usual, with stalls and stalls of stuff. You might not think that's appealing, but for me it's a world of possibility. As soon as I turned down the high street I could feel my mood begin to lift. A smile pulled at my mouth and I walked faster. This was where I wanted to be. This was where I *needed* to be. Chaotic sound and unidentifiable smells surrounded me. *This* was real.

At the end was the fruit-and-veg stand run by

Mick, a tall, bald-headed East Londoner with the loudest voice I'd ever heard. I could always hear him shouting across the street. He noticed me as soon as I approached and chucked me an apple, which landed neatly in my left hand.

"Marty! No school today?"

"Nah, Inset day," I said.

Mick grinned and I could see the large gap between his front teeth. "Another one? That must be about twenty this year. . ."

I shrugged. Mick wasn't going to start lecturing me, though. He knew better than that. Instead he winked.

"You know best, son. How's ya mum doing?"

I felt myself cringe a little – I hate people knowing about her. It was J's fault, always running his mouth off down the pub. I wish he'd keep his gob shut.

"She's good, she'll be home later."

"So, you getting some food in?" he asked. Then his voice dropped. "Tell you what, let me wrap up some bits for you to take back. You can square it with me later. Whadya say?"

I smiled. "Cheers, Mick."

As I walked further down the street clutching a bag with some fruit, carrots and potatoes in, I felt a little better. At least we'd have a little food in the house now, even if I hadn't paid for it yet. I passed various stalls – the clothing rails, mobile-phone covers, dodgy ripped-off designer trainers – until at last I reached my destination: the tiny stall on the corner, run by my second most-favourite person ever – my Aunt Jackie. I walked up to her quickly, my grin bursting from my lips. I could see her various treasures piled high on the table, sparkling silver and bronze.

This stall was filled with potential, because maybe one day it would be mine.

DAISY

Mornings tend to be the worst. There's always this sense of impending panic about the day ahead that seems to whip around us in a horrible, suffocating way. Mum checks the calendar a million times to make sure she has remembered all the appointments and meetings, Dad usually goes into work late so that he can help get Harry ready and I . . . well, I just flit around trying not to get in the way. Trying to help without interfering too much. It's not like I don't understand, because I do. I totally get that everything is crazy for Mum and Dad. They barely sleep and they spend most of the morning in a weird kind of daze. But I guess what's hard sometimes is that they don't seem to notice I'm there. I've become invisible.

Harry always notices me, of course. *His* eyes lit up as soon as I stepped into the kitchen. He had breakfast ages before me, because eating is such a struggle for him – the muscles in his throat are so weak that he could choke any time, and Mum has to make sure his food is easy to manage and that he sits right back in his chair so his breakfast has a better chance of moving down his throat. It's frustrating for him, though. Sometimes, if he is really wound up, the food ends up on the floor or all over us. He throws tantrums and cries for ages, even though he's no longer a baby.

"Daisy!" he said as I walked into the room. I swear his smile could melt the coldest heart.

I ruffled his dark curls. "Hey! You all right, Haz?"

"I'm not hungry!" he moaned. "I want chocolate. Mum said no, though – it's not fair."

"*You* wanting chocolate? *Really?* No change there

then!" I laughed. "Just have another mouthful, hey? Make Mum happy."

I had to admit, the porridge mess in his bowl didn't look too appealing. Actually, it looked more like puke. Harry dug his spoon in and ate a mouthful slowly. Then he stuck his tongue out.

"It's horrible," he moaned.

"Just try. You're doing so well."

He pulled a face and dropped the spoon into the bowl, letting the thick liquid seep over it. Oh well, I did try.

Mum was packing up her bag, which was filled with Harry's stuff, her diaries and things like snacks and drinks. It was pretty heavy – no wonder she complained about her back.

"I'll be home tonight, but tomorrow we'll be at the hospital for another review," Mum said, not looking at me. "Do you want to go to Nan's? I can ask her to drive over."

I hated it when Mum asked this, like she thought I couldn't manage. Besides, poor Nan lived over an hour away; it was hardly a quick trip over.

"It's OK. I have my meeting tomorrow at seven," I said. "I'll just grab something here first. Can you still pick me up after?"

She nodded. "Young carers? I'm so glad you're keeping that up. How's it going there, anyway?"

"It's fine."

In all honesty, I didn't want to go into detail. The group was *my* thing – something that I could do without anyone else. Besides, if I did talk about it, Mum would probably think it was dull. But for me it's just something different to do, with OK people. One of Mum's biggest worries was that I wouldn't be able to cope with stuff, and it made her happy to think I was going to groups and "getting support". The crazy thing was, I didn't need support. I was absolutely fine – I just wished everyone else could understand that.

"Make sure you talk," Mum said, her eyes catching mine. "You must open up, Daisy. It helps, I promise."

"Yeah, sure," I said.

The lie seemed easier somehow.

*

Martha met me outside our form room and we walked in together. This morning she was looking extra good, with her blonde hair slightly curled and swept up in a loose ponytail.

"I have that new eyeliner on," she said, closing her eyes unnecessarily because I could clearly see the dark flick at the corner of her eyes.

"You look *fab*," I told her.

"Seriously?" Martha did her usual wide-eyed *surely not* expression that could be a bit annoying sometimes.

"Seriously. You look amazing. Flynn would be an idiot not to notice."

Her cheeks reddened. "He better notice. I swear, I feel invisible most days."

As we walked into the room I could see Flynn, Martha's on/off boyfriend, sitting on the table at the back of the classroom. He was chatting with Rhys and Danny and didn't even look our way.

"Did he call you?" I asked.

She shook her head. "One text. All weekend. Sometimes I wonder why I bother."

I hesitated while I thought over the options.

Because you're obsessed? Because you like the chase? Because you're oddly attracted to gangly fifteen-year-olds with no sense of humour?

"I don't know," I said instead.

Martha flopped down into the seat next to me. She was blatantly trying not to look at Flynn, but her eyes kept flicking towards him like he had some kind of magnetic pull or something.

"How was your weekend?" she asked eventually, as she dug around in her bag. "Did you and your mum have a nice film night?"

"Yeah..." I said, knowing that my reply was a bit lame. Part of me wished I'd gone round to her house instead. Let's be honest, I might as well have done – after all Mum didn't end up watching anything with me, because she spent most of her evening going up to Harry's room to check on his breathing.

Not that I blamed her. Or him. It was just ... well, how things always were.

Martha was smoothing lip balm on and staring at me with her hard gaze. "'*Yeah...*'? That doesn't sound great. You were looking forward to it so much."

I shrugged. "Harry's so poorly at the moment. His breathing is getting worse at night."

Martha sat back. "Oh no, poor Haz. I'll have to pop over and see him soon."

"He'd love that."

I think Harry has a bit of a crush on Martha. He goes shy and giggly around her. Obviously Martha just finds that even more cute.

"He's the sweetest boy," she said. "I hate thinking of him so ill."

"I know. It's not fair."

And there it was. The heavy feeling in my tummy had come back. Weighing me down. Reminding me nothing was normal. My kid brother was sick and would never get better.

I sucked in a breath sharply and tried to refocus.

"So, this text from Flynn. What did it say? Tell me all the details."

I sat back and let Martha sweep me up into her world of normality.

I liked school because it was a total escape. I could be me and not have to think too much about the other stuff going on. That's not to say that I hated being at home – I didn't. Actually, I *loved* being there. But sometimes it was just too much and everything seemed to swamp me. I'd never tell Mum or Dad this, but sometimes it was as if I didn't belong there. I felt like a spare part. If anything, I was probably something else for them to worry about. So I tried to be quiet. I'd go home, do my homework, play with Harry, maybe help make tea. Then I'd go to my room to give them peace and quiet. I didn't tell them about the thoughts that clawed at the inside of my brain, because I knew they had enough of their own.

When I was younger I used to be more open, I used to tell them stuff. But it was different then. They didn't need to hear my stresses. They had enough of their own.

These days I don't even bother them with the small stuff – I just give them snapshots, tiny insights into my day. I keep it all happy and light. Sometimes I scribble my real thoughts into the back of my diary – deep, dark questions that haunt my mind:

How long will Harry be with us?

What happens if he gets even more ill?

What happens if Mum and Dad keep arguing? Will they split up?

How will we cope if we lose Harry? When we lose Harry...

How will things ever be the same?

What if Mum dies? Or Dad? What happens to us then?

What if I got ill? Who'd look after me?

Writing this stuff down helps a little. It moves everything out of my head and on to the paper. It unclutters my brain for a few minutes. I do all these things because I want to make things easier. I want to be a good daughter. At school I play a different role. I'm top of all my subjects, especially science and English. I wanted to be a vet, which I'd discussed with my form teacher. I was on the school council and I mentored year sevens who were struggling. And I had Martha, who was pretty and loud and meant that I could hang around with some of the more popular girls in our year. At school, people saw me and chatted to me. I had a laugh. I felt part of something. I could shove my worries to one side. Teachers thought I was a great example. They smiled at me in the corridor. They didn't worry about me at all.

Why should they? I got grade As, I was always smiling, I was never in trouble. Who would question that? No one knew that most days I felt like the biggest fake out there. That I was wearing a mask and trying to stop it from cracking and splintering before everyone's eyes.

Did anyone actually know the true me at all?

I walked home the long way. I didn't have hockey practice, so in theory I could've got home on time, but I wasn't ready yet. Sometimes it was just nice to be by myself. To walk and to let my brain empty. I guess it was my way of uncluttering. Usually I cut through the park and walked past the lake and through the small cluster of trees that people weirdly called a "wood". But today I decided to switch direction and pass through the high street. Mum's birthday was coming up and I figured I might find something from the art shop that was there. It was busier than usual, I guess because it was the end of November and people were starting to think about Christmas already. Even the thought of it made me panic a little. Harry struggled with all the chaos.

Would it ever be possible to have a normal family Christmas?

The street was packed with market stalls. I looked up at the lights that were already looped around the wrought-iron streetlamps – at the far end I could already see the green outline of the large tree that was put there every year. I paused for a second, taking in the sight. When I was a kid, Mum and Dad used to bring me to the main event, the switching on of the lights. It was always such a magical evening, seeing the whole town light up like a Christmas dream and admiring the tree as it shone down on us with its thousands of fairy lights twinkling brightly with fake optimism. I couldn't remember the last time we had done that. Mum didn't like bringing Harry out in crowds – or the cold, for that matter. Besides, it would get him overexcited. Even so, I wished—

Someone barged past me, startling me back to

reality. Feeling embarrassed, I began walking again, moving through the crowd of people. The art shop was at the far right of the street, opposite the tree, so I made my way towards it while trying to ignore the temptation of the various stalls. I wished I could let myself just waste some time and browse. It wasn't a big market, just a cluster of traders placed on both sides of the road, with a tasty-smelling burger van sat at the end. I glanced over the menu, my stomach growling, wondering if I had enough money for some chips, but quickly thinking better of it.

I saw the tiny stall then, tucked away in the corner. I guess it caught my eye because it was different. The table itself was draped in colourful cloths, and huge trunks and boxes littered the floor in front of it. I walked over. I could now see that there were loads of interesting things laid out on the top of the table. Antiques, jewellery and a beautiful bronze statue. As I got nearer I saw a small silver box with a purple lid and a butterfly etched on top of it. I reached forward and touched the lid.

"That's a trinket box. Probably from the 1920s," a voice said.

A boy was standing there, smiling at me. I guessed he could only be my age, or a little older. But strangely it seemed like he worked there. He was tall and stocky looking, wrapped up in a dark coat that was too big for him and a scarf that looked as if a dog had chewed the ends. His hair was dark and really scruffy – to be honest, it needed a good comb. His nose was long, slightly misshapen and his skin very pale. But his eyes were what caught my attention. So large and brown like chocolate – they seemed to sparkle like the box.

"It's beautiful," I said. "My mum loves butterflies – I'm looking for a present for her. She likes unusual things."

He smiled. "It's pretty eye-catching. I like it a lot. It's one of my favourites."

"Is it silver?" I turned it over, peering at the base, trying to look like I knew what I was doing. *What am I doing? I haven't got the first clue!*

"No – it's silver-plated. If it was silver it would be

much more expensive. This way you get affordable and beautiful."

I asked. "So how much is affordable?"

His smile widened. "Ah, I dunno... Shall we say a nice round twenty?"

I wasn't sure if that was a good price or not, but as I picked up the box and held it in my hand, it felt good. Like it belonged there. I could imagine my mum putting her earrings in there, or something else precious. This could make her happy, if only for a moment.

"OK," I nodded.

I pulled out my purse and took out the only note left. This was my lunch money too, but it didn't matter. I could beg off Martha for a bit.

He took the note. "Great choice. Would you like me to wrap it up for you?"

"Yes, please." I watched as he found some colourful paper under the stall. As he moved I saw a flash of blue under his coat and recognized the shade instantly. It was our school uniform, St David's. I studied him a little again. It was odd I didn't recognize him, although I guessed he was a year or so older than me. Maybe Martha is right – I *do* spend my life in my own bubble.

He smiled at me again and his eyes seeming to dance with life. Maybe there was something familiar about him but I couldn't quite place it?

"Do you work here all the time?" I asked.

"It's my aunt's stall." He gestured to a small blonde woman who was chatting to a customer at the other end. She was dressed in a long, flowing blue dress and her hair was wrapped in a silk scarf.

"I just help out when I can," he said, wrapping my gift quickly and carefully.

"I bet it's interesting," I said, feeling a little lame. Wanting to ask him more. Really wanting to look in those lovely, dark eyes again.

What's up with you? Get a grip, Daisy!

His head remained bent. "I love it. Antiques, you know... It's my thing. I love working here."

"Funny. I've never noticed this stall before."

He lifted up my box, now wrapped beautifully in blue tissue paper complete with a tiny pink bow.

"That's odd," he said, passing it to me. "It's been

here for years. Maybe something just drew you here today."

I took my present and held it tight in my hand. He was looking at me now, properly looking at me, and I could feel this weird sensation creeping up my spine. It was the feeling that this boy was important to me in some way.

"I think maybe something did," I replied, smiling.

Or some*one*.

I walked away slowly, cursing myself. If I'd had more confidence I would have at least asked his name.

What was it about this scruffy dark-haired stranger that I liked so much?

MARTY

Don't do it. Turn back...

Too late.

I knew she was up as soon as I walked into
the flat – the bad feeling hit me before I'd even
opened the door. As my key slipped into the lock, a
shiver moved down my back. I was used to it, that
uneasy sensation. That knowledge that everything
would go wrong as soon as I stepped into the flat.
Sometimes that feeling was enough to make me
turn around. Go anywhere that wasn't home.

But that was when I wasn't in a good place.

Today I was OK.

Today I could face her.

Just. . .

She was sat in the living room, curled up on the sofa like a tiny kitten. J was on the chair opposite, sitting all stiff and awkward, like he didn't belong there. He jumped up as soon as I walked in.

"Marty! We've been waiting for you. Where have you been?"

I knew I was late – it was past five. My eyes fell on Mum and she smiled weakly at me. She was dressed in jeans and a huge grey cardigan that seemed to swamp her. Was it possible that she had got even smaller in the few hours I'd been gone?

"Hello, Mum," I said, feeling stupid, not really knowing what to say. I glanced at the seat next to her, at the piles of magazines and newspapers, and cursed myself for not cleaning up.

"Marty!" Her voice sounded cracked and wrong, like she was breathing cigarette ash. "I'm feeling so much better now, really I am!"

I walked over and tried not to flinch as she pulled me into a hug. I felt the sharpness of her body. I was scared she'd break in my arms.

"I miss you when you go out," she whispered

into my ear. "I'm so sorry – I never meant for those women to come here. Poking their noses into our business. We'll get rid of them soon, don't you worry."

Tears were pricking the edges of my eyes, but I forced them back. "It's OK, Mum – honestly..." I tried to pull away but she wouldn't let me.

"I'm so sorry. I hate being ill – I feel so useless. But I'm going to get better. This time. I really will – I already feel like I have this new energy."

"Cool," I said.

But will you sleep properly?

Will you eat? Will you really?

Haven't we been here before?

Aren't we just lying to each other all over again?

"I love you, Marty," she whispered, finally letting me go. I could see the redness in her tiny, un-made-up eyes. The wobble in her lips.

"I love you too, Mum," I said, trying to ignore everything else that swamped my brain.

"So, why were you so late?"

Mum was looking at me with fresh interest as

we sat and ate the cheap pizzas that J had picked up from the supermarket earlier. They tasted of rubbery cardboard and I was struggling to swallow mine.

"I went and saw Aunt Jackie for a bit," I said, bending my head and feeling the uncomfortable lump in my throat that was a mixture of congealed dough and honesty.

"Jackie?" Mum's voice was sharp. "Right."

"Jackie's OK, babe," J said, I guess trying to be helpful. "She likes to look out for the kid."

"And your dad? Does she talk about him?"

Now it was J's turn to stiffen. He hated Mum talking about Dad, but what could he do? He couldn't deny his existence – the two of them used to be mates! Anyway, he could hardly get jealous about a ghost, could he?

"No, she doesn't really talk about Dad," I said. "I don't think she likes talking about him too much."

Mum had stopped eating. Her fingers traced the edge of the plate.

"I don't feel very hungry," she said finally, pushing it away.

She turned to face me properly, her cheeks really pink. She was wearing the sulky expression that she often did when she was annoyed with me or wanted something her own way. "Jackie doesn't get it. She doesn't understand, not really. Oh yes, she likes to pretend she cares but she never had a good word to say for your dad when he was alive..." Her voice broke. "Oh, I can't talk about this now. I just don't want you listening to her nonsense."

"I don't," I said, feeling angry now. "I just help her on the stall, that's all."

"Is she paying you?" J's eyes seemed to light up.

"A little."

"See, babe? That's not a bad thing," J squeezed Mum's shoulder. "We could do with a little extra money in the house, couldn't we? Every little helps!"

Mum was slumped back in her chair. She shrugged. "Suppose."

Yeah, you could use the money, seeing as J's not bothering. I might as well be out all day earning. Go on, ask me about my day at school—ask me!

I sat back, pretending to wait for more questions, but of course they never came.

Instead, I nibbled at the crust of my pizza and wondered why this bugged me so much.

Then it was kind of back to the usual routine. I sorted out Mum's meds and ran her a bath with her favourite bath foam – the one that helped her to relax. After that, Mum would usually curl up in front of the soaps and totally zone out. She didn't like much talking during those times – she called it "her rest".

"Do you want a cup of tea?" I asked.

"No thanks, love." Mum smiled. "Honestly, I don't know what I'd do without you."

J had slipped out earlier, no surprise there. He said he was on for a promise of work, but we all knew this just meant he would be playing darts at the pub with his mates. Work wasn't a big deal to J; he just picked up scraps here and there. He always said he hated being tied down.

So that left me and Mum rattling around together in the poky flat, like always. Even though I should've been used to this, it felt odd now. I guess I've got used to having J around.

When Dad was here it was different. He took

charge — he always knew what to do when she was feeling low. He had the answers, or seemed to.

But now he'd left us behind with no clue how to get by without him.

It wasn't fair.

Mum came up beside me. I hadn't realized I had been in a dream, waiting for the bath to fill. The steam was billowing around me in a cloud, choking up the whole room.

"It'll be too hot, love," she said. "I'll need some cold in that — unless you want to give me third-degree burns."

"Yeah, course — sorry." I reached towards the tap.

"You don't have to do this, you know. I'm quite capable of running a bath."

"I know. But I like to."

"I know."

She sounded so sad and I didn't understand why. I watched her as she leant against the door frame. She'd taken off her baggy cardigan and I could see her thin arms even clearer now — like the thinnest branches on baby trees. And her scars. So many of them. Deep, cold lines that reminded us all of the times when she was really hurting. When she tried to get some of the darker stuff out.

But it doesn't work, Mum, does it?

"I *am* going to try this time, Marty," she said softly, her eyes cast down, looking directly at the frayed edges of the carpet. "I've been talking to those women and I've made an appointment with the doctor again. I think – well, I know – that I'm ready to get help now. It's not going to be easy. But somehow I have to break this cycle."

I shook my head. "But we're OK, aren't we? If you just eat properly and rest. Stop worrying so much—"

"No. No, it's more than that. I need to change *this*." She rapped her fingers on the side of her head. "The way I think, react, worry. I let everything get on top of me. Money, stuff about your dad – *everything*. I'm not very good at coping with . . . well, *life*." She drew a breath. Her whole body seemed to shudder.

"I know now that I can do stuff to help that – to help all of us. It'll be hard – but I'm going to do it."

The bath was full. I turned off the taps and

dipped my hand into the frothy water. I always test it, *always*. I've never forgotten the time she got into that boiling bath. She had screamed and cried but refused to move – said the water was cleansing her.

"So many bad things have happened," she said as if reading my mind. "And you've been there for me through all of them."

"Of course I have."

"I couldn't have done it without you," she sighed again. "But I also know now that you need a break. And *you* need help, too."

"Me!" I snorted. "I'm fine, seriously." My mind started whirling back to the conversation the other day. "Hang on. Is this those social workers? Did they talk to you about that daft bloody group?"

"It's not a daft group. And yes, they did speak to me about it." Mum moved into the room, closer to me. She put her hand on my arm. My eyes fell on her skin again.

So thin. Too *thin.*

You're going to break, Mum. Snap in two.

Then what? Then what. . .?

"Please, Marty. I want you to go. I *need* you to

go. It's a chance for us to show everyone that we listen. That we take advice. And it'll help my guilt a little..." Her voice was breaking now. "I've not been a good mum to you, I know that. You must be hurting too. I need to know you are getting all the help you need."

"But I don't want to go to some stupid group."

"Please. For me." Her fingers squeezed my skin, really pinching it. I heard her gasp and realized that she was really crying now.

I sighed. What else could I do? The guilt burnt at me. "OK. OK, I'll check it out, all right? I'll see what it's like. No promises, though."

"Thank you," she said, her voice now lost in her tears. She pulled me into a hug and held me there, clutching me with surprising strength.

"It'll be OK now. It will. *It will*," she said over and over.

I could almost see her words floating up with the receding steam of the room and disappearing in front of me. Lost and forgotten as quickly as they were spoken.

Like always.

DAISY

On the way home from school, Martha was raging about yet another drama in her life. This time it was about Megan and Cara, who apparently flashed Martha filthy looks in Food Tech. They were mates yesterday – obviously this had changed. She was scrolling through her phone as she walked, frowning.

"Seriously – Cara did that slow eye-roll thing that she does, as soon as I walked in the room," Martha huffed. "It's not like she even tried to hide it from me. Then the two of them were huddled up together, giggling the entire lesson. It was doing my head in."

Her scrolling paused for a second. "See! Look at this. Her update. '*Some people drive me mad*' – we all know who she's talking about, the little sneak."

"I'm guessing she saw your post last night?" I said. "She's obviously not happy."

"Maybe," Martha said, now grinning slowly. "But she has to get over that. Her and Flynn were last year, for God's sake. I can't help it that he likes me more."

Even so, I guessed that Martha's rather obvious picture of her and Flynn's selfie – their faces pressed up together and grinning madly – might have been a bit too much for Cara. To be fair it was a bit too much for me and I didn't even fancy Flynn.

"We had such a nice evening together, it was totally worth it," Martha said dismissively. "Why can't I show the world that I'm happy? It makes a change. I deserve a bit of luck."

"Yeah. Of course you do."

I watched as Martha swung into her front gate, her long legs gliding up the path, her eyes totally glued to her screen. "See you tomorrow, yeah?" she said. "And maybe I'll call tonight?"

"Yeah, OK."

She walked in her house without a second glance. It was a lovely looking house, a bit like mine only slightly bigger, an end of terrace. The garden was immaculately tidy and her dad's Audi was parked in the drive. Martha thought she had it bad because she was the only child of two reasonably successful people who both wanted her to do well. They checked her grades and kept her on top of her homework. Martha thought she had it bad because her parents worried about her and wouldn't let her stay out late, especially on weekdays.

Martha thought she had it bad when really she had nothing to complain about.

I realized I had been standing at her gate for too long, just staring at her door and wondering what it was like to be her. I had to stop this. I moved on quickly, checking my own phone and seeing a message from Mum.

Remember I'm late tonight. There's
some frozen lasagne in the freezer.
Don't forget your group. See you at
9pm.

Group tonight. How *could* I forget? It's not as
if I didn't like the group, it was really OK. But
sometimes it just felt like yet another thing I had
to do. Another tick on the list to make everyone
else feel better. I felt tired. I wanted to curl up
on my bed and listen to music – not have Ferry
and Grace teach me another basic skill or try to
"cheer me up" with pointless chat. Anyway, the
group had been offered to me years before, but
Mum and Dad didn't think I needed it then. They
even questioned why I was seen as a Young Carer
at all – *they* looked after Harry, after all – *they* did
all the bad stuff. And to be fair, I did a good job
of pretending that it didn't affect me. But that all
changed when Harry was seriously ill at the end
of last winter. Winter is always a tricky time – any
cough, cold or infection can be a million times
worse for him, and this time he caught a virus that

just didn't seem to shift. And then Mum woke up to find he had stopped breathing again.

It's crazy to think that for some people a simple chest infection can be deadly. Luckily, Harry pulled through. But it was a few days of fear for us. I didn't mean to cry at school. I'd gone in to take my mind off things. But when one of the girls – Tilly, I think – asked how Harry was doing, I just burst into tears and I couldn't stop. It was awful. My pastoral support leader, Mr Fisher, pushed to speak to Mum – and he was the one who said I should be referred to the Young Carers Group. He told Mum that it would be a chance for me to be around other teenagers in a similar position. Have some time out. And I could talk to someone about my worries if I wanted to. I think secretly Mum was a bit put out. Maybe she felt guilty? But she agreed to it, and then she and Dad were suddenly swept up in this notion that they were doing "the right thing" for me and that it would be "good for the whole family".

"We all need a break," Mum had said, taking my hand in hers. I wanted to ask her then why it was so different for her. Why she never accepted the help that was out there. Why she always struggled on. I know Dad was on at her all the time, telling her she needed a break – that there were groups and places Harry could go to – but she wasn't interested. I desperately wanted to know why. But it was never the right time to ask.

As well as getting me involved in Young Carers, Mr Fisher also put my name down for the school counsellor. I was still waiting my turn for that, and I was pretty relieved I hadn't had to go yet – I only agreed to do it to shut everyone up. I didn't actually want to do it. There was only one counsellor, a lady called Emily. I wasn't sure that I *ever* wanted to talk to her. What would she know, really? How would going over it all ever help me? The thought of opening up about my life to a complete stranger was bad enough – but the fact it would be about Harry was just too much. I didn't want to keep going over and over the same old stuff. The only thing that would help any of us was if they found a cure for Harry. And that wasn't going to happen – not in his lifetime, anyway. I knew the facts, and

I had to learn to deal with them, just like my mum had. But there was one fact that was slowly killing all of us: my little brother was sick and he would never, ever get better.

Ferry was at the door as soon as I walked into the youth centre. As usual it was freezing cold in the hall, so I kept my coat on, pulling it even tighter around my neck.

"Daisy! On time as usual. How have you been?" he asked, as he checked my name off the list.

"Yeah, not too bad," I said, smiling up at him.

Ferry was one of those people who was really hard not to like. He had to be in his late thirties, or thereabouts, but he acted much younger. He was tall and lanky with cropped dark hair and a goofy grin. He was also smart enough to know that I didn't really want to be there, but he always made me feel so relaxed that it was hard not to kind of enjoy it. Besides, I figured out that it was easier to chill out while I was there than it was to be all moody.

Ferry and the other leaders didn't expect us to talk about stuff – not if we didn't want to. And that suited me fine. When I started coming to this group I thought it would be so heavy, with a load of us sitting around in a circle talking about "problems". But it wasn't like that at all. Actually, it was the polar opposite. They know here that most of us didn't want that. We just wanted to escape.

"We're having quite a relaxed session tonight," Ferry said. "Now it's December we're getting some dropouts. Coughs and colds, I expect. Willow isn't here tonight, neither is Jack."

"Aw, that's a shame."

I really liked Willow. She was a year older than me, but super friendly. Her dad had MS and Willow had to do a lot to help him, as her mum worked full time. I wondered why she wasn't there – I hoped everything was OK for her at home.

"Marvin and Harvey are in there. And Amber. Some of the others should be arriving in a bit," Ferry said. "Go grab Grace, tell her you're here."

I pushed open the heavy wooden doors and walked into the main hall. The cold always felt a bit worse in here. The hall was like a giant echo chamber – the sound bounced off each wall. I could see Marvin and Harvey at the far end, bouncing a basketball between them. The steady thuds travelled across the room. Over on the stage some younger lads were playing on the Xbox and yelling at each other. At least they weren't on the drums today, not yet, anyway.

Grace was perched on a small table, chatting to Amber and her younger sister, Chloe. I probably liked Grace the best out of the leaders. She was young, too – maybe twenty – and she just seemed to *get it*. She understood what it was like to be one of us. Everyone liked her, especially Harvey and Dean who obviously fancied her. I flopped down on one of the small, squat chairs next to them. It was dead comfy even if it was falling to bits.

"Hey!" I said, announcing my arrival.

Chloe looked up first. She was quite new to our group and only eleven. I think she had been in the younger group before and had just moved up. Her tiny blue eyes darted towards mine and looked away quickly. She was quite shy. Amber beamed at me, as always. She was dead friendly and outgoing, and usually the first up to play football with the boys.

"All right, Daze!" she said.

"Hey, Daisy. Good to see you!" Grace smiled. "Amber, Chloe and me have just been chatting about Christmas. It's so exciting and so stressful at the same time."

"Tell me about it," I muttered.

"My mum and dad are saying we might go away," Amber said. "We don't know if this will be Mum's last ... well, we just don't know. We want to make it a really special one for all of us."

I looked over at Amber, at her soft features. She wasn't showing signs of being upset, but I could almost see the heaviness that she carried inside her. Her mum had been fighting cancer for months. I couldn't even imagine what that was like. I think Chloe was struggling more. She usually had her head dipped and her face was very pale.

"I'm sure it will be special," I told them.

Grace nodded. "Course it will. And what about you? Any plans yet?"

I thought about the last argument I'd overheard between Mum and Dad. How Dad had insisted that his family come over for the day and Mum had begged him for a quiet time with just us. She was getting so tired and stressed lately; I couldn't even begin to imagine how Christmas would pan out.

"Nah," I said evenly. "No plans. So anyway – what are we doing tonight?"

Grace's large brown eyes studied me for a second, and then she nodded and glanced away. "Well let's see... Do either of you fancy a game of pool before the rabble arrive?"

It was nice not having to think too much – just laugh and act silly for a while. No one judged you or made weird comments here. There is this understanding that we treat each other with respect – we had enough grief at home, we didn't need more here. In a weird way, we just acted like kids. We could be free. Normal. At one point, Callum – one of the older boys – started chasing us around the room like a loon. It was like being five years old again, but in a nice way. We could shout, cheer and make noise without thinking about the other stuff.

We could be light for once. Free.

So if nothing else, this place was different. It was a release.

As I got up to leave, Grace moved towards me. She was holding a cup of tea in her hands and her face had that pinched look that she often wore when she was concerned and wanted to talk.

"You sure everything's OK, Daisy?" she said softly.

"Yeah, course." I picked up my bag. "Why wouldn't it be?"

"I dunno. You just look a bit tired. And our chat earlier about Christmas – you seemed keen to change the subject."

I shrugged. "I stayed up late last night chatting to Martha, that's all."

"OK. Just make sure you get some rest tonight, yeah?"

"Yeah."

"And I'm here if you need me."

I nodded and made my way towards the door. As I pushed it open, I realized there was someone behind it, so I stepped back to let them through.

"Thank you," he said, walking in.

I didn't look up straight away, but when I did I was taken aback by who was in front of me. I stepped aside a little, trying to hide my confusion.

"Hey. We meet again," he said.

I was standing face to face with the messy-haired boy from the market. Not only was his hair still messy, but he was also still wearing that shabby old coat. Then he smiled, and his whole face seemed to change. I felt something light up in me.

"We certainly do," I said, grinning.

MARTY

So, some guy called Ferry had rung earlier in the day and asked me to meet him at the Youth Centre. He reckoned that would be a good time for me to go through the forms for the Young Carers Group.

"I would normally come to your home," he said. "But I understand your mum has only just got over a bug of some kind?"

I thought about Mum sitting in the living room, listening to our conversation. The thought made me baulk. "It's OK. I'll come to you."

"Cool. Come at nine, if you like – the session will be finishing up and we can have a quick chat. I can tell you a little bit about what we do and get you to sign some forms. You're lucky, there's usually a huge waiting list but I've just had some older kids move up."

"Yeah, sure," I said. Lucky? Seriously? I felt like the least lucky person right then.

I jotted down the address, even though I didn't need to. The centre was just across the estate, about a ten-minute walk from the flat. I wouldn't even need to get a bus.

I looked down at my scrawled notes and sighed. Was this my social life now? Some rubbish meeting in a run-down hall? I wondered what the hell I was going to be facing. A room full of whinging kids moaning about their lives while nibbling biscuits, holding hands and pretending to care about each other, maybe? How the hell was that meant to help anyone?

It was all complete bull.

Of course, Mum was on my case immediately, rushing into my room to check I had taken the call, probing me for details, making sure I knew exactly where I was going. Sometimes Mum liked to act like a mum, even though we both knew she'd actually given up that role years ago. Given up, or forgotten ... I guess it amounts to the same thing.

"I'm sure it'll be fun," she said in that fake-happy way of hers. "You might make friends."

I cringed. "I don't make friends, Mum. That's not going to happen."

She didn't know about me. She didn't know about my reputation. She still remembered me at five years old when I used to go to birthday parties and play football matches on the rec. That wasn't me any more, and she didn't even know.

"Just go in with an open mind," she insisted. "Sometimes things can surprise you."

"I'm going, Mum. Quit stressing."

What I didn't tell her was that I planned to go to one or two sessions and then sack the whole thing off. I had better ways to spend my time.

But she didn't need to know that.

I got to the centre a little early, so hung around outside for a bit like a total loner. It was biting cold, and I had to keep moving – pulling my coat up and around my jaw to stop the icy breeze clawing at my neck. I couldn't see much through the window. A couple of lads were sitting down, talking. Someone else was at a table – writing, maybe? It looked dull. I turned just as the door on my right slammed shut. A tall guy with a huge afro strode out. He paused when he saw me.

"Hey, peeping Tom. Looking for someone?"

I shook my head. "Nah. And I ain't no peeping Tom."

He laughed. "I'm just messing, bruv. No need to get stressed." He strolled over. "I'm Harvey. You joining the group? Ferry said there was gonna be a new guy."

I shrugged. "Maybe. Just checking it out."

"It's OK, you know. Quite chilled. Gets you out the house." He smirked. "And I'm happy to get out of my house any day of the week right now."

"Whatever," I mumbled, glaring at him. I wasn't interested in his life.

Harvey nudged the side of my arm. "Hey, good luck with it. Maybe I'll see you next week?"

Then he walked off towards the bus stop. He was so tall, his stride was loping and fast.

I watched him for a bit and let out a resigned sigh. I made my way through the same door he had just exited.

There was no one in the hall, and it felt weirdly colder in here than it had outside. The place smelt musty. I moved towards the two double doors in front of me, my shoes squeaking on the floor as I did, and as I pushed against one I realized someone else was coming through from the other side. I quickly stood aside to let them pass, but they did the same thing. It could've gone on for an age so I stepped through the door. I recognized the girl instantly – she'd been at the stall a few days ago. She wasn't someone I'd forget in a hurry. She had long reddish bouncy hair and dark glasses that seemed to suit her round face perfectly. As soon as she smiled I saw tiny dimples pop into her cheeks, and noticed the tiny gap between her front teeth.

She's cool. Really *cool.*

I said something lame – the words falling out my mouth like they always did when I wasn't thinking – and she replied but I didn't hear because

I still confused. How was she here? I'd thought about her long after I saw her at the market. I never thought I'd see her again.

"Marty?" A voice boomed across the room. "I'm so glad you found us OK."

A man who I could only assume was Ferry bounced towards me with his arms outstretched as if he was about to embrace me. I stepped back, unsure. I wanted to talk to the girl but as I turned to say something, I saw her back as she walked out the door. It slammed loudly after her, the noise echoing loudly.

"So. I'm hoping you still want to join?" Ferry said, his arms by his side now but a smile still resting on his overly happy face.

My thoughts were still with the girl. I didn't even know her name. How could I find it out?

I turned back to Ferry. "Yeah," I said. "I still want to join."

Twenty minutes later we were done. Ferry shook my hand and shoved all the forms into his bag.

"It'll be good to have you here," he said.

I half nodded. "Yeah, well ... It's something to do, isn't it?"

"Yeah. I guess it is." Ferry grinned.

I turned to go.

"See you next week, then," he called.

"Yeah ... yeah. Next week."

I ducked out of the room, feeling strangely awkward. It wasn't as if the conversation had been too weird, if anything Ferry had been pretty relaxed. But maybe that was the problem? There was something about his casual approach that made me want to sit with him longer. Talk to him. Tell him how things really were. I shook my head quickly. Was I some kind of nutter? I'd never get social services off my back if I did that.

I pushed the main door open, letting the evening air blast my face. It felt good, like a shot of reality. I was awake now, thinking clearly. These groups, these sessions, they made the professionals feel like they were doing something helpful, but no one really understood. Unless they were me, how the hell could they? I started jogging down the path, figuring it was the quickest way to get home. I'd been out for about an hour now and although J had promised to come back early, I bet he'd not bothered. I didn't like to think of Mum sitting there alone. When she was by herself, she starting thinking, worrying, doing odd things. She needed me with her. I kept her safe.

"Hey!"

I looked around quickly and saw her. She was sitting on the low wall to the side of the building. She looked so cold, huddled up in her small coat, her legs drawn up towards her and her arms wrapped tightly around them, one hand clasping her phone.

"It's so cold," she said, like she could read my mind. "My jeans are so thin, it's like I'm wearing paper."

I stared back at her. Was she for real? "Well, if you're going to sit on a wall in winter..."

"Smart-arse. My mum is late picking me up. I could wait in the building I guess, but I can't see the car from there." A small frown rested on her face. "She knew the time... I've just tried calling and she's not picked up. Hopefully she's on her way. I didn't think she'd be late today."

I walked over to her. Then, sighing, I shrugged off my bulky warm coat. "Here, I can't have you sitting there like that. You'll freeze. Put this over your shoulders."

"Oh God! No! You don't have to do that. You'll get cold."

"Seriously, I don't feel the cold. I quite like it, actually. Probably comes from years of living in an unheated flat. Here—"

I placed the coat over her. I was suddenly aware of how tatty it seemed against her and I cringed a little. "I'm sorry it's a bit old, I just—"

"It's fine," she snuggled into it, smiling. "Thank you."

We stood there for few seconds just smiling. I guess it was a little awkward, but not in a bad way. Gently, I sat down next to her, making sure there was some space between us. I didn't want to look like some sad creep sitting right on top of her.

"You're what my mum would call a proper gentleman," she said softly. "Are you sure you're not cold?"

A gentleman. No one has called me that before!

I guess I was a bit cold now that I was just sitting there in a T-shirt. But I didn't mind.

"It's OK. Honestly."

"So..." Her face tipped towards me a little. "Are you going to join our little group?"

"I guess," I said. "I mean, this sort of stuff isn't really for me, but I don't have much choice."

"Choice? What do you mean?"

I sighed. "It's complicated. Let's just say other people are involved. It's not exactly how I would choose to spend my time."

"Oh." She nodded. "I get it. That's not easy."

The streetlight was shining down on us, and I could sneak tiny glances at her, really noticing how pretty and cool she seemed. There was something about her. I couldn't pinpoint what it was, but I could tell she was special. She seemed, I don't know ... unique.

She shifted slightly, like she could feel my thoughts again. "My mum will be here in a minute. She has to be. It's nearly Harry's bedtime."

"Harry? Is that your brother?"

"Yes. He's not well. Hence..." She gestured.

"Mum gets distracted sometimes. And so does Dad. It's ... well, you know. It's tricky."

"Yeah – I know..."

As if on cue a car swept into the car park, its headlights blinding us for a second. She smacked her hands together.

"At last! I was seriously thinking of calling a cab."

I stood up quickly. "I'm glad you're getting home OK."

She pulled the coat off her shoulders, her fingers delicately folding it before handing it back to me. "Thank you so much... Oh my God, I don't even know your name!"

"Marty," I said.

"Marty?" I could see her process that. "That's so weird, my favourite film has a Marty in it."

I laughed – I couldn't help myself. "*Back to the Future*! It's my mum's favourite, too. She watches it all the time."

"That's pretty weird." She smiled as she began to walk to the car. "Hopefully I'll see you next week, Marty?"

"Yes. I think so..."

"Daisy!" she called over her shoulder. "My name is Daisy."

"Ha!" I called back. "Another coincidence – that's my favourite flower."

Luckily she seemed to work out I was joking and not being a total weirdo, and she smiled in return. "Yeah, right!"

I watched as she stepped into the car, leaning over to say something to the driver. Then the door slammed and the car reversed.

"Daisy," I said under my breath.

Daisy.

It was a nice name.

And not such a bad flower either.

I stayed on the wall for a while, her name floating in my head. She was caught inside there. I wanted to find out more.

DAISY

I yelled at Mum as soon as I got in the car. I couldn't help it. The words just seemed to explode out of me like fireworks.

"Where were you? You knew I was here tonight."

Mum pulled out of the car park, a grim look set on her face. But she wasn't answering me. That made me even more cross.

"You forgot, didn't you?" I yelled, the accusation hanging between us.

"No, I didn't forget." Mum's voice was strangely calm. "And I'm not going to talk to you while you're raising your voice."

I sank back into the seat, feeling like a sulky

child. Outside the lights of houses sped past. Already people had started to put Christmas decorations up and they shone brightly, almost begging me to start feeling festive.

Well, they could just shut up...

"Harry's appointment dragged on," Mum said finally, her voice still flat and cool. "They had a lot to tell us. I needed to pull myself together a bit before coming to get you, that's all. I wanted to make sure I was OK to drive."

That didn't sound good. The familiar heaviness sat in my stomach. "What is it? What did they say?"

"Oh, more of the same. Harry's muscles are getting weaker. He'll need steroids, and the side-effects aren't great..." Mum's voice trailed off. "It wasn't as if we *weren't* expecting to hear it, but I guess you never give up hope, do you? And I *always* hope that he will stabilize, or things will turn around, but..."

Her voice broke. I could see her hands shaking on the wheel. She gripped on tighter. It was times like these when I wished Dad could drive, but he loved his motorbike so much he never got round to learning.

"Tell me about tonight – tell me something nice," she said. "What did you do?"

"Oh, more of the same, really. I beat Gracie at pool, and chatted to some of the others. It was really nice tonight. But lots of people didn't come."

"The cold keeps people away."

"Maybe. A new boy joined. I think he's a year older than me. He goes to St David's, actually. I talked to him outside and he seems OK. Different. A bit moody, but OK."

I wanted to tell her how much I liked his face, how he had looked glum at first but then suddenly expressive and cheeky. I wanted to tell her how he'd given me his coat and sat shivering next to me. I think that's the kindest thing any stranger has ever done for me. But I didn't say these things, because I also wanted to keep them to myself, this was my private stuff, something I didn't need to share and discuss.

I liked him. Just really liked him.

"It must be hard joining the group so late when

friendships have already formed. You found it hard enough," Mum said as we turned into our drive.

"I guess."

It *had* been hard at first, but nowhere near as bad as I'd imagined. I'd stressed about it, thinking it would be like joining a new school, that I'd be the outsider and immediately shunned. But even from day one it was clear that the group operated differently. Everyone was welcoming. No one was judged.

It's a good group. I like it, despite my early reservations. And it has really helped me.

Mum pulled up on to our drive. She switched off the engine and took a deep breath. All the time her eyes were fixed on the house.

"Are you OK?" I asked.

"Sometimes it's hard coming back," she said, and her voice sounded so lost, like she was far away. Her eyes stayed glued on the drawn curtains. "It's just too hard."

Harry was sleeping. He looked so cute when he was asleep – a proper angel, with red cheeks, and dark hair stuck to his face. His eyelashes were pressed against his skin so you could see their length. He was a noisy sleeper, making tiny pig-like snuffles.

Next to his bed was the chair where Mum often sat and watched him. We had the monitors, but it wasn't always enough for her – when she was really worried she would curl up here next to him. Dad would beg her not to, tell her she needed sleep. But Mum wouldn't listen.

"Hey, little fella." I brushed a kiss on his cheek and he barely flinched. "I missed you today."

I hate not seeing him. Time with Harry is precious. Every second. And even though I hate his condition and what it is doing to our family, I love Harry with all my heart. He can't help this. He's the result of some crappy faulty gene. He didn't ask for it – he's just my kid brother with the cutest smile and the deepest snores I've ever heard.

"Night night, smelly bum," I whispered into his ear, breathing in his slightly salty smell. "Sweet dreams. See you in the morning."

I kiss him goodnight every night – it's my ritual.

If I kissed him and wished him sweet dreams, everything would be all right for another day.

I padded out of the room and on to the landing. As I approached the stairs I could hear my parents arguing in the living room. I walked halfway down and sat on the step, feeling a tightness pull through my body.

Dad's voice was loudest. "...You *know* that's not fair."

I could tell he was really upset.

"I'm just telling you how I feel, that's all. You asked and I'm telling."

"But to *blame* me..."

"I'm not blaming you!" Mum's voice was louder now. "This isn't about you!"

"Of course it is! You're implying I don't do enough! I work *full-time*. Then I work *overtime* because we need the money. I can't be here as well, Nat! This was what we agreed. If you need more help—"

"I don't want strangers with Harry. That's not fair on him."

"But you need to consider it, Nat. If you're this

tired and stressed. At the moment I have no choice but to work."

"I know we need the money. I know that! All I'm saying is everything is on top of me. The appointments, the caring, the insomnia... I feel broken."

Broken? I shrink back, feeling sick. Mum can't be saying this. She was the strength of our family. She held us all together. I could hear crying now, the soft sobs of my mother filtering through the walls. Each one seemed to sting me.

"It's too much. Too much! The little respite I have... I can't do this. I can't. And all the time knowing..."

I could hear Dad mumbling, but not his actual words.

"But it is!" she said, louder. "It's all my fault..."

I leant in further, trying to hear more.

"If it wasn't for me, he'd be healthy..."

I spent most of the evening shut away in my room. I didn't want to see Mum's tear-stained face or listen to her make up more excuses for not being straight with me. Did she think I couldn't handle it?

She never talked to me about these things, not any more. Those awful overheard words kept replaying in my mind.

It's all my fault.

How could she feel to blame for Harry? It was a fluke, just one of those things. Why was she being so irrational?

I messaged Martha. It wasn't that I wanted to talk about stuff going on at home – she didn't need to hear that. But I wanted to focus on something else. Martha was always good at diverting my attention.

I'm blocking loads of people online, she typed. Still getting grief from those crazy bitches. Had enough now.

Yeah. Maybe you need a break, I replied.

How did it go tonight?

I read her question and thought for a second before tapping out my reply.

OK. Same as ever, really. New guy came. Think he's in the year above us. Marty?

She seemed to take ages to reply. I scanned my room while I waited, wondering when would be a good time to tell Mum that I wanted to redecorate. The faded pink paint and frilly curtains were looking a bit lame now. I longed to slap some nice bright colour on to the walls.

Finally, her message came through.

Marty? Marty Field? You serious?

I stared at it, confused.

Yeah, well I guess so? Don't know his last name, but there can't be many Martys?

Her response was much faster now.

Hang on, I'm calling you.

I sat back on the bed, clutching my mobile wondering what the big deal was. Martha was such a drama queen sometimes. My phone began to buzz.

"Daisy, I swear sometimes you live in a little world all by yourself." Her tone was light and she was laughing a little. "This must be the same Marty. Messy dark hair, tall, looks totally scruffy, always scowling – how do you not know about him?"

I sighed. "I dunno. He looked a little familiar, but I'm not great with faces and I don't go round staring at people like you do. What's the big deal? He seems nice enough."

"He came to our school late, joined last year I think. But barely bothers to show up now, so I guess you won't have seen him as much. But he's in the same form as Emmie."

"Oh."

Emmie was Martha's cousin. Most of the time they pretended they hated each other, but I think secretly they were more similar than they liked to admit.

"Anyway." Martha took a deep breath in. I could

picture her sat back on her bed with a grin plastered on her face. She loved to gossip, it was what she did best. "According to all the stories, Marty Field is a complete nutter. Like, he can come across all sweet and charming, but then lose it at the smallest thing. Emmie told me once that he was quite popular in his old school, everyone thought he was all right. Then at the end of year nine, one of his mates said something to him – it was just banter, nothing serious. But Marty just lost the plot."

"Really? What happened?"

My stomach felt like it was lined with lead. Did I really want to know this? I wasn't sure I wanted to go there, but a nagging voice was telling me to listen.

You want to know who Marty really is, don't you? You need to know...

"I'm not quite sure, but I know he hurt the other kid pretty bad – so bad that the police were involved and stuff. He was temporarily excluded, but that school, Greenfields, were pretty fed up with him – I think he was getting into trouble before that, too. Emmie said there was talk about him losing his dad around the same time – maybe that was what made him a bit crazy. He was moved to our school in the end, probably to stop him getting permanently excluded. No one goes near him. He's so weird."

"That's awful." I thought of the boy sitting next to me in the cold. I couldn't imagine him being violent or nasty. But then again, I didn't even know him – how could I even begin to know what he was capable of?

"Anyway, Emmie says he's odd and still a bit scary – and you know Emmie, she's not scared of anyone. I think he bunks a lot. He probably hangs around with those dropouts on the estate."

"You don't know that," I said, feeling a shot of anger.

"Well, what else would he be doing? He's dodgy and he lives round that way, in the flats. There's loads of them like that. I bet he'll only be at your group for a couple of sessions. He's probably only going because he has to."

"We'll see."

"But he's not like the type of guy you'd hang around with, is he?" Martha giggled. "Seriously, could you imagine? His hair would drive me mad. You need to get to know that Harvey more – now he's hot!"

"You met Harvey *once*, Marth. And he's got a girlfriend. And he's not my type."

"So what is?"

"I dunno."

But as my thoughts drifted off, I couldn't shift Marty from my mind. I didn't care about his scruffy hair – it was kind of cute. And I remembered the way his smile seemed to change the entire look of his face. Why was he so angry? And why did he make *me* grin every time I thought of him?

I wanted to know more about him.

MARTY

Seriously ... enough already.

Mum was singing along to the radio when I woke up. Some bloody Christmas song. Even the *thought* of Christmas made my stomach sink. How were we going to manage this year? I couldn't even face talking to her about it. Not yet.

But her singing wasn't the only thing to surprise me. She had ironed my uniform and hung it up on my bedroom door.

Jesus, was I seeing things?

I sat up in bed and stared at the saggy shape of my greying clothes. I wasn't sure it was possible to hate a uniform as much as I did. Just looking at it made my muscles clench as if they were in a vice. It was a bloody straightjacket. A way of marking me and keeping me in a place I hated. If it was possible never to set foot in St David's again I would be happy.

But what choice did I have? I sank back on my pillow and let out a groan. Nothing was in my control – nothing. Everyone was making decisions for me. How was that even fair when it had been *me* keeping this family together for so long?

Why couldn't they just leave me alone?

As if on cue, there was a light rap on the door and Mum burst in. She was already dressed in a low-cut red T-shirt and jeans. Her blonde hair was straightened and her face made up. She looked . . . *nice*.

"Good, you're awake," she said. "I've got some toast here. And tea. Have it quick, you don't want to be late."

"I need a shower," I moaned, pulling myself up again. "How come you're up so early?"

"I'm seeing the doctor again," Mum sighed. "Not that I need them. It's a total waste of time, but that stupid cow of a social worker insisted. I was just run down before – that was all. I feel much better today."

Much better today. How many times had I heard *that* line?

"You can't be late today," she continued, walking around my room, picking up my clothes from last night. It was doing my head in. I didn't like her touching my stuff. "You must show them, Marty. I don't want any calls. No letters – OK?"

I wondered if the school had tried to ring her about my absences. Mum had changed her mobile number recently, to stop the debt collectors calling. I told her I'd given it to the school but of course I hadn't. I didn't want them giving her grief. But the letters would come soon, I was sure of it. I couldn't hide it for long.

"I'll go into school today," I said, knowing full well that I could go in for registration and then slip away again – they'd hardly notice I was gone.

She smiled at me, bright and trusting. "It'll do you good – getting out of this flat for a bit."

Her thin arms pinched around her body as

she clutched herself tight. "Sometimes it feels so claustrophobic in here – don't you think? It's almost like the walls are pressing in."

I shrugged. Apart from being cold and damp most of the time, the place was all right. It was a place to be.

I got up quickly, running a hand through my hair. Reaching for my stuff, I went to shower, but Mum stood in my way.

"When did you get to be so tall?" she asked, her voice lighter now, her hand reaching up to stroke my face.

I flinched. "I've always been tall, Mum. Stop being daft."

"You're shooting up." Her hand fell again and hung by her side. "You look so much like him now, Marty. Every day I see him in you. You're his image."

I gently eased my way past her. "I need a shower, Mum."

"He loved you so much," she whispered, just loud enough for me to hear. I slipped into the bathroom and locked the door quickly behind me. It was only once I was standing under the lukewarm water that I could finally unclench my fists.

I'm not like him, I think, as the spray and tears sting my eyes. *I'll never be like him.*

If only I was.

Of course I was late again, but this was part of my plan. I took my usual detour past the local shop and then walked the longer route to school through the park. Although it was still cold, the day was bright and dry and the only other people around were a couple of dog walkers and an enthusiastic jogger. I glanced at my watch and worked out that if I arrived ten minutes after everyone else then I might get another late warning but would still be registered. More importantly, I would avoid the crowds and kids like Josh Falmer who would only get in my face and wind me up.

As I approached the school, the usual heaviness descended on me. I looked at the grey building and wondered why it had to resemble a prison block. Everything about it was *bleak*. It represented unhappiness and containment and I loathed it. My legs were primed to run – to head in the opposite direction – but I had to stop myself.

Slowly, I walked through the wrought-iron gate and dragged myself up the path that ran alongside the playground. A few stragglers stood by the goalposts on the other side, probably sneaking a quick fag. Other than that it was fairly quiet. I looked up and saw that Mrs Richards, one of the science teachers, was standing at the main doors, marking in the latecomers. She smiled as I approached.

"Martin. I've not seen you in a long time." She began to write my name on her sheet.

"It's Marty, I've never been Martin," I said, for probably the hundredth time in my life.

"Oh." She obviously wasn't that interested and as I leant forward I noticed she had still written "Martin" down. "So. Why are you late?"

"Only by ten minutes, miss."

"Ten minutes is ten minutes," she said in a weird formal way that didn't seem to suit her. She had a friendly, smiley face. I bet she hated doing door duty really – I bet she wanted to be in the staff room with the rest of them, hiding in the warm.

"I got lost," I said, smirking. "Took a different route and it threw me. Can I please go inside? I wouldn't want to miss out on my education."

"There's no need to be smart with me, Martin."

"Marty. And I wouldn't say I'm smart," I said. "But instead of me, you might want to concentrate your attention on those smokers over there."

She turned to look where I was pointing and while she was distracted I slipped past her.

My smile disappeared and the heaviness returned.

Seriously, a lot of it doesn't bother me at all. I don't care that none of the others sit with me. I get it. If I were them, I wouldn't want to sit with me either. I chose to sit at the front of the lessons, well away from the popular lot. I can still remember how it used to be at my old school. How I used to be the one having a laugh, feeling part of a crew. I look at kids like Josh, who's in most of my classes. He totally hates me – I know it. You can tell by the way he looks at me. But he's one of the cool kids, the one everyone's meant to like. He's funny and smart and pretty hard too. I *should* want to be like him. I *was* him, once.

Now I'm no one.

Sometimes, I listen to the lesson. Other times I drown out the noise of the room and just switch off completely. All the words, the information – it clogs my head up. Does my head in, depending on my mood. Sometimes I'm just not interested. I want to be somewhere else, doing other things.

In maths, Mr Nelson was going on and on – throwing figures into the air like they were some kind of fairy dust. On the board behind him was this long equation, and he was desperately trying to help us work it out, trying to make everything sound magical and exciting when in fact it was dull and repetitive. I felt like tiny maggots were working their way through my nervous system and into my muscles, making me want to get up and move. The only way I could relax myself was to put my head on the desk and zone out.

Of course he came over, slamming his long white hand on the wood in front of me, making me jolt.

"Marty! Am I keeping you up?" he boomed.

At least he got my name right. I lifted my head

and frowned up at his huge, round, angry face. We'd never liked each other. Mr Nelson had marked me out as a troublemaker from early on and I'd marked him out as an idiot.

"We are working on a complex equation here," he barked, glaring down at my sheet. He leant in a little. "You haven't even made a start on the work? Have you been listening at all?"

"I've been trying," I said.

"Trying? Really?" He lifted up my paper. "And this is trying?"

I glared back at him as I sat back in my seat. Behind me I could hear giggles. Someone said, "Watch it, he's going to kick off any minute."

My skin prickled.

"I don't like this attitude, Marty. You come back into this class after absence. You're obviously behind and you're making no effort. I'll need to speak to you after the lesson."

"Don't bother," I said, picking up my bag. "I'm not interested."

Mr Nelson snorted in disgust, a sort of "well that's just typical" noise. I turned to walk out, listening to the murmurs and sniggers behind me. I shot a filthy look at Josh.

Maybe we could've been mates if things had been different. Now he was just glaring back at me, daring me to say something.

"You know what, sir?" I said as I walked past. "I didn't need to listen because I already know the answer. X is four. I worked it out as soon as I walked in."

I enjoyed the look of shock on his face as I left the classroom, closing the door quietly behind me.

I wandered the corridors for a bit, not sure where to go. I had planned on going outside and chilling out behind the science block, but it had started to rain and I didn't fancy getting wet. I knew Mr Nelson would have alerted a senior teacher and they would probably be looking for me. They all had radios and walked around the school like special agents, buzzing each other when they picked up some rogue kid. Weirdly, today it looked pretty quiet out and about. Maybe I'd be left alone.

I found myself walking into the drama

department, which was part of the old bit of the school building, and quite dark and musty. From the far room I could hear the noise of a lesson going on. Outside there was a kid sitting on a chair. He looked up at me as I walked past.

"What did you do?" I asked.

He had a sulky face and a line of spots around his mouth. "I called the teacher a bitch."

"Ah. Not so smart." I peered through the glass to see who was taking the lesson. Miss Green – she was actually one of the cool ones. "Mate, you've got that wrong."

"Yeah, well. I lost my temper."

"I know that feeling – what are you, year nine?"

"Ten."

I was surprised – he looked much younger. All weedy and pathetic sat there. I peered through the glass again. A few looked vaguely familiar. But then again, I was hardly here nowadays. This had never been my school. Then someone caught my eye. The flash of red hair, the glasses.

"Hey, is Daisy in your class?"

"Daisy Morgan? Yeah, why?"

"Just wondering."

I kept looking. I couldn't quite stop myself – even though it was a bit weird. A bit stalkerish. She was standing in a small group to the side and was laughing. Her whole face was bright and alive. I really wanted to go in. Watch her properly, hear her speak.

"Do you know her then?" the boy asked.

My eyes scanned her as she moved across the room, easy and light, her hair bouncing off her shoulders. "Nah, not really. What's she like?"

". . . OK, I guess. Smart. Quite funny. I don't really hang around with her."

I moved away from the door and studied him again. "No, I guess you wouldn't."

"Do you want me to say anything to her?"

I started to walk away, feeling a bit happier for some reason, although I couldn't say why. "Just tell her a friend looked in on her. A *gentleman* friend."

And hopefully she'll remember she called me a gentleman for giving her my jacket, otherwise I'll sound like a complete tool.

*

Mr Terry didn't want to sit down with me in the office. Instead he suggested that we go for a walk. "I need a breather," he said. "It's been a long day."

We ended up walking along the path that ran parallel to the playing field. I was meant to be in French but Mr Terry had called me out. There was a rugby match going on and the shouts from the game were breaking up the silence between us. I found myself watching them as we walked past. I'd never really been into rugby – football used to be my thing, once. But I hadn't kicked a ball for ages.

"I thought we should have a chat, Marty. You know I'm concerned about you."

I trudged along beside him, not really having much to say. I liked Mr Terry – he was OK. But I didn't want him making a big deal out of stuff.

"What happened in maths today?" he asked.

"I walked out. Mr Nelson was doing my head in."

"That's not a reason to leave a lesson, you know that."

"I just couldn't deal with him going on and on." I sighed. "It's too easy. I know all that stuff already."

Mr Terry slowed his pace a little. "I know. I

get that. But, Marty, your attendance has affected your grades. You're a natural at some elements of maths, but other sections you have missed entirely and are behind in. We had to move you down a set. We explained this all to you."

"I'm here now, aren't I?"

"Yes and I'm pleased about that. But you haven't been here and that's the problem. Since you joined the school in year ten, your attendance has been below seventy per cent. It's shocking. The only reason your mum has escaped a fine is because of your situation. We all understand how hard it's been."

"Our situation?" I stopped walking, turned to face him. "We're fine, me and Mum. This is nothing to do with her."

"But Marty – it is, can't you see? Every time you miss school there is a chance the county council could contact your mum and take her to court. She'll end up with more worry. Also, don't you think she wants you to do well in school? You're a bright kid. You can turn your life around."

"I'm not bright," I snapped.

Dad thought I was bright, that's why he got me into Greenfields in the first place. He appealed and fought to get me a place there – the best school in the area. And look what happened. I screwed it up. I guess that proved even Dad got things wrong sometimes.

"You've been through a lot. It's no wonder you've struggled, anyone would," he insisted. "But it's about looking forward now."

We were stood there – the pair of us in the cold afternoon sun – Mr Terry squinting down at me with a soft smile on his face and me feeling like I wanted to punch him or hug him. Maybe both. It was a weird, unsettling feeling. I could feel the pressure building inside me again. I clenched my fists and quickly uncurled them. The longing to pull away from him, to run, was almost overbearing. I had to look away – force myself to focus on the rugby match and the shouts and cries over there.

"Remember, I'm always here," he said.

I started walking, but this time back towards the school.

"I can't make any promises," I said quietly over my shoulder at him.

"I just want you to try," he replied, his gentle words cutting through me.

I nodded.

I would.

But I honestly wasn't sure how much longer I could keep this going for.

DAISY

Eddie Palmer grabbed my arm as I was leaving drama. He was possibly the most irritating kid in our year, so I immediately flinched away from him. Thankfully, that morning he'd spent most of the lesson parked on a chair outside rather than making smart comments in the lesson in an attempt to wind everyone up.

"You have an admirer," he said, his grin showing a mouthful of unbrushed teeth.

I pulled away from him. If this was his way of making a move, he was going about it the wrong way. Behind me Lizzie and Leela giggled. I wanted to puke.

"Oh man," Lizzie whispered. "This could be interesting."

Eddie pouted his lips a little and tried to stand a bit taller. I actually felt a bit sorry for him. "No," he said. "It's not me, is it – as if!"

"As if!" laughed Leela, and I quickly elbowed her in the ribs.

"It was that kid from year eleven. The weird one," he continued, glaring at us all.

"Oh, he sounds HOT!" cooed Lizzie.

"Yeah, you wanna track that one down," Leela said, grabbing my arm. "Come on, we'll be late for lunch."

"Did he say anything?" I asked Eddie, who was now moving back in the drama room, ready for his lecture with Miss Green. She looked in a proper mood; he was bound to end up with a week of detentions.

"Nah – just something about telling you a gentleman called." He shrugged. "He's a weirdo and hardly a gentleman."

Gentleman? My skin prickled. It had to be Marty. Who else would've said that? I grinned.

"C'mon." Leela grabbed my arm, pulling me down the corridor. "You're not seriously listening to that freak, are you? He's probably making it up."

"Yeah, I know," I said.

But I hoped he wasn't.

In the lunch hall I looked around for him, but couldn't see Marty at all. To be fair, most year elevens went out for lunch, but I still thought there was a chance I'd catch sight of him. This guy was invisible though. It was like he didn't exist at school. He was like some kind of ghost student, with rumours that he haunted the school, but only some chance sightings.

I was sitting with Martha on a table at the back of the room. Usually we'd be with the larger group, but Cara was on that table and it was pretty obvious from the looks we got that we weren't welcome there. Martha was still ranting about the unfairness of everything and how everyone was now taking Cara's side over this Flynn business. It was getting a little repetitive, if I was honest. My concentration was slipping.

"You're looking for him, aren't you? That bloody

Marty Field?" Martha said, slipping out of her rant. I turned back to my lunch of soggy chips and bread. Strangely, I wasn't that hungry. "Nah – just thinking," I muttered. "I'm not looking for anyone. What were you saying?"

"Nothing. Just that Cara is a stuck-up, toad-faced skank. Or maybe that's too nice." She took a bite of her sandwich and studied me. "Seriously, you *were* looking for him. I could tell. I know you!"

"I dunno. I just thought I might see him in here, that's all."

"Yeah well, I told you he's a basket case. You should check out Simon Davies instead. Suddenly that boy has grown some muscles!"

I smiled. "Last year you were calling him a freak."

"A girl can change her mind!"

Martha was certainly gifted at that. I watched as her eyes trailed the room. She marked people out, made quick decisions on whether they were worth her attention. Sometimes this annoyed me and sometimes I found it amusing. I knew Martha was only really doing it for show; she liked to appear hypercritical and cold. That wasn't her at all, though, not really. Martha had been a rock to me over the past few years. It had been her that had sat with me when I was feeling low or worried. She would come over and babysit with me, if Mum and Dad were having an evening out. And she was amazing with Harry. Some people treated him like he was made of glass and were a little awkward in his company — but Martha just acted like there was nothing wrong, tickling him, teasing him and chasing him around the room. As a result, Harry adored her.

"You need to talk to Cara," I said finally. "Megan was posting this morning, saying you two are going to fight." I stared at her. "You're not seriously going to fight over some boy, are you?"

I expected her to laugh and tell me not to be silly. But her face remained serious and her eyes were now fixed on the other table. On Cara, who was laughing loudly like she was the happiest person in the room. Martha eye-rolled and took a bite of her sandwich. "She's just being dramatic. But if Cara keeps mouthing off behind my back, I won't put up with it."

"But you can't fight her. Martha, this isn't you!"

Cara was someone who got into fights – she was known for it – but not Martha. Martha could hurt you with her words – could flash you an evil stare from a million miles away – but never this.

Martha sighed. "But I like Flynn. Cara needs to understand that. I'm not giving him up."

"So just talk to her."

"I'm done talking," she stood up, staring down at me. "Sometimes talking just isn't enough."

The rumours circulated all day, building up momentum like a storm. I could hear people behind me in lessons, whispering.

There's going to be a fight – Martha and Cara. Outside school today.

My head was aching. I really didn't want to get involved in this sort of stuff; it totally wasn't my thing. Before last lesson, I caught up with Martha outside the art block. I pulled her to the side. "Walk another way home," I hissed. "Don't get involved in this."

Martha stared back at me, her eyes hard and cold. "No. I told you. I'm not running away. I'm walking my usual way and if you're any type of mate you'll walk with me."

I flinched. I didn't want to be dragged into this, but at the same time Martha was my friend. I could hardly leave her to deal with this alone.

"You're crazy," I said.

"They're just throwing threats around. It won't come to anything – but I have to be seen to front it." She sighed, pushing her fringe out of her eyes. "It'll be fine, I promise. It's no big deal. Just meet me at the end of school."

She strolled into her lesson without even waiting for my reply. I stood there for a moment. This was a big deal. To me, anyway. I could hardly get involved in some stupid fight – if the school found out, my parents would be called and I would get so much grief from them. Did I really want to stress them out even more?

But as I made my way back over to English, I knew I couldn't let Martha down. She'd always been there for me. Maybe she was right – maybe this was just some big storm that would calm down soon enough. Just words being slung around. Idle threats.

I had to hope.

The lesson passed in a blur, without me paying much attention. I could still hear whispers but I chose to ignore them. My head felt crowded enough without filling it with more worry.

Under my desk I looked at a picture of me and Harry on my phone. It had been taken a few months ago. He looked so cute and smiley, his dark curls pressed up against my podgy face. We didn't look that alike but we had the same smiles, the same dimples in our cheeks. In this shot you wouldn't think anything was wrong. You would just see a boy on his sister's lap, laughing at the daft joke she'd just made. You wouldn't know that a few hours after it was taken, Harry's legs had given way in the living room and he'd cracked his head on the corner of the TV stand. You wouldn't know that he was rushed to hospital and I spent an hour crying in Martha's arms, terrified that he'd hurt himself beyond repair. You wouldn't know that it was Martha who made me feel better, Martha who got me through it.

No one knew this stuff except me.

The bell rang. I grabbed my bag and went to meet her.

"She'll be waiting for us on the path towards the shops," Martha said, her bag slung casually over her shoulder. She was trying to look relaxed but I could see she was chewing her lip hard.

I knew the path she meant. There had been fights there before because it wasn't overlooked. I tried to avoid walking that way, preferring to take the longer route across the housing estate.

"What has Flynn said about all this?" I asked as we started walking.

"Not much. I think he thinks it's funny – you know, girls fighting over him."

Yeah, I bet he did.

"Didn't he tell you not to bother? I mean, he must think it's pointless. Can't he talk to Cara?"

"Cara won't listen to him. She just wants to make a point, that's all. She thinks she's the hardest girl in the year, but I'm not going to be pushed around."

"You used to be mates..."

We *all* did.

"Yeah, well, that was before."

Before Flynn and his amazing sex appeal arrived on the scene. I still couldn't see the attraction. OK, he was good-looking, but that hardly made up for his bad attitude and arrogance. But it was no good telling Martha that, she was so stubborn. Once she'd made her mind up about something, that was it.

I remember in primary school when someone had called me a baby for crying when Mum dropped me off. Of course they didn't know that I was scared about the stuff that was happening at home, stuff I didn't fully understand. Harry had only been a baby but he had been so ill. Martha was the only one who did know and she thumped the kid who teased me. She also refused to apologize.

"They're in the wrong – why should I apologize?"

It's just how she was.

We came to the middle of the path, where it turned sharply towards the shops. I immediately saw Cara sitting with some other girls in our year – Willow and Emily. Cara tended to switch friends quite a lot; she wasn't particularly loyal. She grinned when she saw us. It was a snake-like expression that changed her face into a cruel mask.

"So, you didn't back out..."

Martha stayed where she was, one hand still resting on her bag. "Why would I?" Her voice was cool and measured.

"I see you brought back-up." Cara's small piggy eyes looked me up and down. "Although I can't say I'm that impressed with your choice."

I felt my cheeks burn. She was right. What the hell was I even doing here? The best thing I could do was run and call for help, and I couldn't even run that fast.

Cara stepped forward. "So – it's quite simple, you either dump Flynn and cut out the comments about me, or..."

"Or what?" Martha pulled herself up. "What are you going to do?"

Cara's hand flashed out in a second, grabbing a handful of Martha's blonde hair. She tugged, dragging Martha down towards her. Martha was flinching, trying not to shout out, but I could see her face paling.

"You seriously want to ask that question?" Cara screamed. "Do you know what I'm capable of?"

"Oh, not much, I'd imagine," said another voice.

I hadn't seen him before and didn't know where he'd come from, but suddenly Marty was behind me, staring at Cara with what looked like amusement in his eyes.

"I'd let go of her if I were you," he said. His voice was light, but there was something in the tone. Something that hinted at a deeper threat.

Cara was staring at him, her hand still gripping Martha's hair. "What the *hell* has this got to do with you?"

"Everything. Now let go of her and get the hell out of here."

Willow stepped forward. "Cara, man. Leave it."

Her eyes flicked over to Marty. She looked scared.

Cara let go of Martha and stepped back slowly, wiping her hands on her skirt. "What are you? Their protector, or something?"

"Maybe," Marty smiled. "And it was a pleasure meeting you. But I think you should go."

Cara's eyes flashed at Martha, who was busy rubbing her head. She picked up her bag.

"I'm not leaving this. You still owe me."

We watched them walk off down the path. I could hear Cara arguing with Willow. I turned to Marty.

"What was that all about?"

"I was just helping," he shrugged.

"They were scared of you."

"Of course they were. They know who he is," Martha said. She was still rubbing her head and looking at Marty suspiciously.

"Yeah, well, you shouldn't believe everything you hear," he said as he turned and carried on down the path. I wanted to call after him, but something stopped me.

"Why did he rock up like that?" Martha asked.

"I don't know," I said.

And I really didn't. But I wanted to find out.

MARTY

So, throughout the week Mum had gone from zombified to totally hyped up and motivated.

Great.

First she decided to rearrange the living room and then she started bagging up clothes that she decided she didn't need any more. At first it was OK. I convinced myself that she was trying to change things and keep herself busy, but I could only keep that lame idea in my head for so long. We had been here before, of course. Lots of times before.

The nights were the worst. I'd hear her up until late either watching horror movies on TV or tapping away on the internet, sometimes talking to herself and shouting out something random. J wasn't around, either. He'd taken some labouring job down near Brighton and said he'd be away for a few weeks. I couldn't blame him – we needed the money. But he didn't look too upset to be leaving us, either.

"Just take it easy, yeah?" he said to Mum, before giving her an uneasy kiss on the cheek and scarpering. I could almost see the relief drip off him as he slammed the door. Part of me just wanted to tear off after him.

Please, mate, just take me with you...

Mum didn't care. She was too absorbed talking to her friends online. Her eyes would zip up and down the screen while her fingers tapped away erratically. I wasn't sure what she was even looking at. She'd done this before – like last year, when she'd got involved with some debate about bloody breastfeeding. This stuff seemed to keep her busy. But I couldn't help noticing how pale her skin was getting, and how the circles under her eyes were growing bigger and darker. She kept telling me she was fine, that she'd been to the doctor's and he'd signed her off with a clean bill of health. But how could that be true? Wouldn't the doctor have seen the same shabby-looking woman that I did?

"The government is lying to us," she told me, as I tried to make us both toast one morning. "They lie to us all the time. We are conditioned to believe what they say, but it's rubbish. It's all there – the truth is all out there."

"Really?" I handed her a plate, willing her to at least take a few bites this time.

Mum nodded, but she wasn't listening. Her mind was elsewhere. Putting down the plate, she scuttled back to the computer.

"The lies are everywhere," she called at me. "They don't want us to know, but we do. We're rising up – we're rising up against them."

I walked behind her, glancing at the screen. "Mum. Seriously. Maybe you should take a break from that for a bit."

"I'm fine."

Beside her, the phone buzzed. She physically flinched, then we both moved towards it.

"Don't. I've got it," she hissed.

I watched as she checked the screen and swiped her finger across it, rejecting the call.

"I know their game. I know what they want from me," she muttered, stuffing her phone into her pocket. Her face was pushed into an angry frown.

"Was that social services?" I asked.

"Maybe..." She shrugged. "They can wait. I'll call them back later. It's not important – I think they'll sign me off soon."

Really? I hoped so – the thought of those women picking through our lives again made my blood run cold. But, seriously, was she well enough?

"Will you be OK?" I asked, and my words felt hollow. She was already lost in her online world, her mouse moving the thread back and forth. Beside her, the toast was going cold. It would probably stay there all day.

"I'll be fine," she said, her voice bright. "I have lots to keep me busy."

As I left, the guilt clawed at me. Deep down, I knew how this would end up. And once again I felt powerless to stop it.

So I went to school, because that felt like the

only thing I could do. For Mum. At least I lasted two periods this time.

I wanted to make it through the day – I tried to convince myself I could. But Josh put a downer on that. I shouldn't have cut through the canteen at break – it's always too crowded and noisy. But I did, and that was my mistake. Josh was in front of me in seconds, charging towards me at speed. I knew he was going to knock into me and tried to move out of the way, but his barge still caught me. And his drink tipped over my blazer.

"Oh! I'm sorry, mate!" he said, fake sincerity oozing from him, like pus from a spot. He stood back and his group of pathetic loser mates started laughing. "I probably did you a favour, though. Looks like you need a new uniform anyway?"

I didn't need to look at my sleeves to know they were too short, or to see that the colour was fading.

I stared Josh straight in the eye. "That was out of order."

"And what are you going to do about it?" he growled, the smile still stuck on his ugly face.

I shoved past him, this time getting satisfaction in knocking him sideways and hearing the tiny gasps from around the room – ripples of excitement: the lunch hall had woken up. Josh said something and then swore, but I'd had enough. I wasn't going to perform for these dumb idiots.

I was out of there.

I headed straight to the market, as always. I'm not saying the bad feelings go away, it's not like that, but most of the time I can switch off if I'm at the market, and that helps a bit. I guess it's like I'm being someone else for the day. I'm not some kid with a mental mum. I'm Marty the smiley-faced lad with a knack for antiques – or so I'd like to think. It was Dad who got me into all this. He used to have this stall before he died and Jackie took over. Everyone here knew and loved him. Being back where he was helped me feel that connection again. Mum can't understand that because she doesn't like to remember, it hurts her too much. But here on his stall, I can somehow remember him without feeling pain. This was my favourite place to be at weekends and holidays. I loved his laugh when he made a good sale, his insistence that everything needed to look just right when we laid it out. The best thing was the long chats we would have during the quieter times, perched on frayed stalls and drinking tasteless tea from the burger van. Dad taught me all he knew. He always said he wasn't very bright, but what he did know, he knew *well*. He knew where a piece of silver was from by looking at its hallmark. He could tell the difference between a proper painting and a print without removing it from the frame, and he could reel off names of designers for glass, ceramics and pottery.

"Some things – some people – make the world that little bit brighter, more beautiful," he'd say, and he was right.

Now it was Jackie who sat on his faded blue stall. She shared a similar bright smile, but she didn't have the same passion. She was always pleased to see me, though, and would wrap me up in one of her suffocating hugs every time.

"Why are you not at school?" she asked as soon as she pulled away.

"Free periods," I replied. I always told her the same things and she couldn't be bothered to argue. I knew Jackie thought it was better having me here, where she could keep an eye on me, than wandering the streets. She'd tried talking to Mum about it, but Mum always told her to mind her own business so now Jackie had given up trying to argue.

"Marty, your blazer!" She grabbed my jacket, making me flinch. There was still a stain all down it and it would probably stink later. But it was fine. I didn't care.

"It's OK." I pulled away. "Leave it, please."

"Give it to me," she gestured with her hand. "I'll wash it at mine. You can't expect—"

The words hung in the air. I knew what she meant. I shrugged off my jacket and handed it over.

"You need a bigger size," she muttered. "I'll talk to Jo."

Yeah, good luck with that. I imagined Mum still at home, busy with her new project. I doubt she even remembered she had a son right now. Jackie gave me a job pricing up some tea services and plates that she'd picked up in a house clearance the day before. It was good-quality china but not very old. As I laid it out carefully I tried to remember the last time she had picked up anything quality. There was no way she'd make much money on this.

"You should let me come next time," I said.

"What, and get under my feet even more?" she chuckled. "You do need to be at school some days you know."

"I know, but—"

"No buts. Just put that service out."

I carried on, feeling a bit defeated. I had my box of stuff at home – little treasures I'd picked up in charity shops and sales. I *could* offer it all to her ... but it was mine – my starting block for when I took over.

"Look for jewellery next time," I muttered. "And anything silver. It always sells."

"OK, smarty-pants."

She stood up and moved towards me, immediately overpowering me with the smell of floral perfume and stale cigarettes. Her arm was heavy and awkward around my waist as she gave me a quick squeeze.

"I worry about you," she said. "You're like my own. I know Joe would be so proud."

I kept my head dipped, suddenly not wanting to talk about Dad.

"How's your mum today, anyway?"

"She's keeping busy. Reading things on the internet and ... I dunno, you know Mum."

"Yes. I do know your mum," she sighed. "Has she been to the doctor again? I still think she needs that counselling."

"She said she's been and they signed her off. They think she's doing all right."

But that was only what Mum said – who knew the truth? She'd lied before. And I could see from Jackie's pinched expression that she didn't believe it this time. That said everything.

"And the social?" Jackie whispered the words, as if she was swearing. "Are they still on your case?"

"I'm not sure. I know Mum has meetings. I think they'll see me again soon, too."

I thought of that phone call she ignored earlier

and prayed that wasn't them. "If we can just show them we're OK, they'll leave us alone."

"Well. They *are* very busy."

"We don't need them, Jackie. Mum's been up and down but she's doing OK now."

Jackie moved aside a little. "I wish she'd let me come over, but she's never liked interference, has she? At least when Joe was alive he could keep her ... well, happy. I guess losing him has hit her the hardest of us all."

Has it? He was my *dad.*

"You know you can come to me whenever you need to, Marty? Yes I'm a bit out of town, but I *am* here for you."

I blinked hard, moving the plates to the far side of the table. I was still thinking on Jackie's words. *Had* Dad's death hit Mum the hardest? Most of the time she lived in her own little world. No one had actually asked me how I felt about it – any of it. But he was *my* dad. I took a deep breath and focused on the antiques. Bright and shiny.

"Beautiful things make us happy, Marty..."

But they don't, Dad. They're just things. They

lie to us. They pretend to be something they're not. They can't fix us; they can't mend us. They can't bring people back.

"Are you OK, sweetheart?" Jackie's hand was on my back. "You *do* know I'm here for you? I'm always here."

"I just can't..."

The words were tumbling awkwardly from my throat. I lifted my head to look at her, but she was already looking away. Her bright grin was now switched on for a customer.

Feeling stupid I stuffed the loose newspaper back in the cardboard boxes under the stall, listening to the conversations above me. I took a few gulps of air and tried to refocus. If I concentrated – really concentrated – I could still picture him standing there. Right in front of me. And what would he be saying?

Pull yourself together, lad. We've got a job to do.

I felt a bit better about going to the carers meeting later that day. I'm not saying that I was desperate to be there, or anything – the whole thing still felt a bit pointless and annoying – but

I knew Daisy would be there and that was worth showing up for. I hadn't seen her since last week in the alleyway. It's not as if I was going to admit it to anyone, but I was waiting to see if I could catch sight of her. I don't know what I was thinking, really – maybe that I could just bump into her and make conversation. It was pretty clear that something was going on though, you could tell by the way her mate was acting – almost dragging her along and talking loudly. I guess I just followed them to see what the fuss was about. I hadn't expected to run into some girl fight. Well, it was impossible *not* to run into it – I could hear the shouting from miles away. And the way Daisy looked... I'd immediately felt sorry for her and wanted to take her away from there. She'd looked so uncomfortable – you could tell she wasn't used to situations like that.

Seeing her again just made me more interested in her. It was a weird feeling. And when I was at school I found myself looking for her. Dad always said he liked Mum the minute he met her at a party when they were teenagers. He said he heard her laughing and was caught like a fish on a line. He always said that Mum was the best thing in his life. But Dad was a soppy old romantic. I never thought I would be. That soppy crap is for other people. Not me. Surely not me...

As soon as I walked into the room, my eyes were sweeping the place looking for her. It was pretty full already. In one of the rooms, some lads had taken over the drum kits and were knocking out a relentless beat. Across the hall from them, others were kicking a ball around. A tall kid with blond hair turned as I walked past the open door.

"Hey, fancy a kick about?" he asked.

The guys that were with him were also looking. I guessed they were younger than me. The blond boy was smiling and looked all right, but the others seemed a bit hostile.

"Maybe later," I said.

"You new? I've not seen you here before."

God, I was the new kid again. I remember how I felt that first day at St David's – how the rumours had done the rounds before I'd even started. They'd all known what I did, and it was like walking into a play with a part that had already been set out for me. I couldn't even try to start again – my role was clear. I couldn't be anything else.

It felt the same here, and I hated being on the outside *all the time*. These guys were staring at me, already trying to work me out and it made me feel sick.

"I'm just here for a bit, you know." I tried to keep my voice casual. "Trying it out."

"Oh," He nodded. "Well, I'm Jack. Grab me for a game later, if you feel like it?" His grin seemed real. He returned back to his mates, who were no longer looking at me, and I suddenly felt stupid and a bit harsh.

"Yeah – er, thanks," I said as I shuffled into the next room. This was the one Ferry called the "chill-out zone" where people could talk or use computers, or even watch a film. I liked it better in here. A couple of people were sat around chatting, but luckily Ferry was at the door. He fist bumped me as soon as I walked in. "Hey, Marty! Good to see you!"

And as I chatted back to him, I noticed Daisy.

She was in the corner on the sofa with a girl and a boy. She looked up and waved me over.

"Cool," Ferry said, grinning. "You know Daisy. And that's Tia and Leo – they're brother and sister and have been coming here since they were kids. They'll help you settle in, no trouble."

I nodded.

Yeah, I thought. *Hopefully they will.*

Daisy laughed a lot in the group, and she talked a lot too. Not about herself but about all kinds of things. She had lots of opinions and insights into the way the world was and what she wanted to do about it. Listening to her was both exciting and exhausting.

"Don't you want to travel?" she asked us, after explaining her plans to trek across Europe. "Don't you think you owe it to yourself to see the world? I feel so cooped up here."

I thought of our tiny flat – the claustrophobic space where Mum and me existed – and nodded.

"Yeah, I guess... Sometimes."

"We both want to travel. Maybe after university," Tia said. "There's so much I want to do and Dad says we should take our opportunities when we can."

Daisy was grinning. "Exactly! My parents did all this before I was even born. They bought some old banger and drove across America. They said it was amazing – one the best things they've ever done."

I sat back on the sofa. It was soft and spongy and dead old, like something you would find in an old people's home.

"My parents never left this town," I said. "And maybe I won't either. Sometimes it just works out like that. It doesn't bother me."

Daisy turned to face me, her cheeks were pink and she looked a bit cross. "It doesn't have to be that way," she said. "You can do what you want with your life. Choose to go where *you* want."

"What with?!" I leant forward, keeping my voice calm. "I mean – what am I going to use to fund this exotic trip? I'm not being funny, but we haven't exactly got money floating around."

"Neither have we," said Daisy. "But I'll still make it happen."

"Good for you," I replied.

She shook her head, her face looked so serious. "But you must have dreams, Marty? Ambitions?"

"Of course I have. I'll leave school and set up my business," I smiled at her. "And I'll buy my mum the nicest house I can. I'll look after her."

Daisy nodded. "That's a pretty cool ambition."

After a moment I replied. "It's not my ambition. It's my reality."

After the session, I waited outside with Daisy again. She didn't seem to mind, and this time she'd brought a coat. We stood by the door to keep a little warmer. Her eyes were mainly fixed on the car park, but she kept flicking tiny glances at me. She seemed nervous.

"Honestly, you don't have to wait with me," she said. "Mum won't be as late this time, I'm sure."

"I don't mind – it's fine. I only live over there," I pointed absently towards the grey housing estate in front of us. "It's hardly a long walk."

"Quite close to school then," she said. "But I heard you went somewhere else before?"

I shifted a little. "Yeah. Well, my dad got me into Greenfields but it didn't quite work out."

"And you never come to school..."

"I don't think school suits me," I muttered.

"Sounds like a cop-out to me. If you went to somewhere like Greenfields, you can do well at St David's. You just can't be bothered."

"It's not like that." My skin was starting to prickle.

"What *is* it like?"

"I dunno..." I looked away, towards my estate. My home. "Everything changed after Dad died. I don't want to deal with things like school. It's like my mind has jumbled up. That stuff's just not for me."

There was silence then, like neither of us was sure what to say next. Daisy was shifting her feet beside me and I couldn't tell if it was because she was cold or just feeling awkward, because her head was dipped and she'd turned away from me.

Then she coughed softly and spoke again. "I'm really sorry about your dad. I can't even begin to know what that would be like."

She sounded sincere and her hand brushed my arm and then quickly moved away again. "Would you believe my dad wanted me to go to St David's even though it's further away from me? It's his old school and he wanted me there."

"Where do you live then?"

"Milton Avenue," she paused. "It sounds posh but it's not really. My house needs doing up badly."

I grinned. Milton Avenue was on the other side of town and it was *really* posh, all detached houses and neat driveways. "You should see my gaff," I laughed. "A poxy sixth-floor box in the Griffin tower block."

She glanced over at me. "I'm sorry, I didn't mean to sound ungrateful. It's just our house is a wreck compared to most on the street. When my parents bought it they were doing OK, you know? But then Mum had to give up her job..."

"I get it," I said quickly. "You don't have to explain."

"One the girls from my year lives in your block, the one you saw fighting the other day? Cara. She's in number twenty-three."

I nodded. "I thought she looked familiar. I'm higher up, number thirty-three." I paused. "And what was that fight about, anyway? It all looked pretty lame!"

"Oh, it was my best mate, Martha. She's going out with Cara's ex, so they've fallen out big time. I guess I just got dragged in."

"You don't want to get involved in stuff like that."

"And you would know all about *stuff like that*?" Her eyes were bright. She was testing the ground. She must've have heard things.

"You don't want to believe everything you hear," I said softly. "There's a lot of rubbish flying around."

"I can make up my own mind," she said. "Besides, I—"

We saw the beam of the headlights swing into the car park, followed by the crunch of gravel. Her mum was here again, and I was immediately disappointed. I wanted more time — I wanted to hear what she was going to say. I wished her mum had been late again and then regretted the thought, knowing that would've just made Daisy upset.

Daisy picked up her bag and tucked a tiny strand of red hair behind her ear. The light through the door made her skin seem even more delicate somehow, like the best china on my stall. Her lips were curled into a perfect smile. When she looked at me, I swore she didn't see the waste of space that everyone else seemed to. She saw someone else. And I didn't feel uncomfortable with her.

"I'd better go," she said, a little awkwardly. "It's been ... nice."

"It has." I hung back, unsure what to say next. I watched as she moved away, her curls bouncing against her coat.

"Daisy!"

She turned, looking back at me, her expression confused. She stepped back a little, casting a nervous glance to her mum in the car.

"Could we ... I don't know, meet up after school? I mean, we don't have to, I just thought..."

My words were spilling out and making no sense; my cheeks were burning. Why was I so crap at this? I sounded like a year seven kid begging for attention.

Daisy just shrugged, like she was cool with it all. "Give me your phone."

I dug out my battered mobile and watched as she punched her number in.

"Message me. We can walk home together."

"That'll be cool."

"It'll mean you'll have to go to school, though," she said, and her eyes sparkled.

"Maybe..." I took my phone back, lightly catching the skin on her hand as I did.

"No 'maybe'. Go to school and we'll meet up. That's the deal," she grinned again, moving away. "I'm not hanging around with some dropout."

"OK, OK."

She nodded. Then turned and walked away.

It's hard to judge a nod, but if I *was* going to, I would say that was one of the nicest ones I'd ever seen.

DAISY

Harry was sitting on the floor beside me, his chubby body pressed up against mine, one hand clutching his beloved cuddly dog, Dudley. Mum was in the kitchen sorting out the evening meal. I brushed my hand across the pages of his book, pointing out the carefully drawn illustrations. This was his favourite story. I had read it to him over and over and we both knew it off by heart, but Harry never got bored.

"I like your funny voices," Harry giggled, resting his head on my lap.

This was how I liked it – just us. Doing stuff that normal brothers and sisters did. And Harry was good today. His cold had eased and he seemed to be walking without too much pain. I could almost imagine. . .

I squeezed my eyes shut. *Don't do this. Don't.*

Beside me my phone buzzed.

Harry lifted his head, his eyes gleaming with excitement. "Is Martha coming to see us?"

I laughed. "You love her so much! Hang on. . ."

I swiped the screen and saw it was a number I didn't recognize. I paused for a second, the breath catching in my throat.

"Well, is it? Tell her to come! I've not seen her in ages!"

"No, Harry, it's not Martha. . ."

She's too busy with Flynn. . .

I opened the message, trying to resist the cheesy smile that was bursting out of me.

Hey, it's me, Marty! Just wanted to say cheers for the chat. I'm going to school tomorrow, so shall I meet you after? Let me know.

I could almost hear him saying the words, all awkward but like he was trying to be casual. It was sweet, somehow – not at all like this tough guy I'd been told he was.

Harry was tugging my arm. "Who is it?"

"Just a boy from my group, that's all. No one special."

Harry giggled again. "A *boy*? Do you have a boyfriend?"

"No! Don't be silly!"

I tapped out a quick reply, trying not to overthink it. This was me being my very best super-cool-and-relaxed self.

That sounds good. See you at the main gates at 3.30?

"You've got a boyfriend!" Harry shrieked, sitting up and pointing. "You have!"

"I haven't!" I lunged at him, tickling his soft belly. "Just because you have a million girlfriends doesn't mean I have a boyfriend."

Harry shrieked in pleasure, kicking out his legs. "Aagh, get off me. Get off!"

I didn't see Mum walk back in the room; it was like she just appeared. She pulled my arm away from Harry, and her grip was *tight*. Too tight.

"You can't do that, Daisy!" Her words were brittle. "You could hurt him."

"It was fun, Mummy." Harry's red little face stared up at her. "We were just playing."

"It wasn't playing, it was reckless," Mum said, her dark eyes staring into mine. "And Daisy should know better."

Why was I always disappointing her?

My mum and dad didn't even bother to hide their argument this time – in fact it was so loud I was surprised the whole street didn't hear. Poor Dad got verbally attacked as soon as he walked through the door. He was only half an hour late, but Mum lost it.

"You didn't call, Chris," she yelled. "How can I get dinner ready if you don't tell me what's going on!"

Dad was shrugging off his jacket. "I had to finish something at work. It's no big deal." He was looking so tired lately – his cheeks were drawn in and shadows hung heavy under his eyes. He walked over to Harry and pulled him into a hug. "How's my little lad been?"

"How do you think?" Mum's voice was spiked

with rage. "He cried this morning when his legs gave way again on the steps. His muscles have been hurting this afternoon. It's not been a great day."

I thought that was unfair – this had been a better day for Harry, but Mum was so angry. Dad didn't say anything back. I watched as he buried his head into Harry's hair. He just looked so sad.

"He's OK, Dad," I said. "We had a nice afternoon, didn't we, Harry?"

Harry nodded. Dad looked up at me and smiled.

"That's good," he said. But he sounded lost, like he wasn't quite with us at all.

"It's lucky I had Daisy after school. How else would I have got anything done," Mum said. "I'm functioning on no sleep, the house looks like a bombsite and you think it's OK to drift in when you please."

"I can't just leave work at the drop of a hat. I'm needed there, too." Dad's voice was rising.

"Of course you are," Mum hissed.

"I don't understand what this is about. *I have to work*. We need the money. We agreed this was the best way. One of us had to keep working."

I thought of Mum before Harry got really ill. She had worked as an analyst like Dad and had loved her job. I remember how the two of them used to talk about work things over dinner and laugh. She had been so different then.

"I know one of us has to work," Mum said, her voice flat. "The problem is, the other one gets left behind."

After that, I took Harry upstairs. I didn't want to hear the constant bickering and even Harry was ratty and refused to settle properly. Mum ended up snapping at him and stomping out of his room. I crept in after her and sat on the end of his bed. I liked it in Harry's room. It was full of bright lights and soothing objects. A space mobile hung from the ceiling, fairy lights shone around his bed and glow-in-the-dark stickers plastered his wall. Harry was buried deep under his duvet; I could only see the top of his head.

"Mum is shouty," he said, his voice all muffled.

"I know. She's tired."

His face peeked out, pale and glowing slightly in the dark room. "Is it because of me?"

I stroked his cheek, not really knowing how to answer. Harry had never asked a question like that before. He usually seemed to be oblivious to all the stress around him.

"I think she worries about you, but she'll be OK," I said softly. "Sometimes parents just get angry with each other. That's what happens."

But it had been worse recently. Even I couldn't deny that.

"Is she excited about Christmas?" Harry's voice lifted, obviously excited at the thought.

I tapped his nose. "Of course she is! Not long now – you better be good!"

Harry giggled. "I'll will."

"Maybe I'll ask Mum if we can put up the decorations this week – what d'you say?"

"Yes!"

"And you can write your letter to Santa. You haven't done that yet, have you?"

"No, but I know what I want," he whispered. "Can I tell you?"

I leant in close. "Go on, then."

"An Xbox to play games on, a puppy, a bouncy

ball and. . ." His breath was warm against my skin. "I'm going to ask Santa to make my legs work properly."

I wasn't going to cry – I couldn't. This wasn't about me. Instead, I kept a smile plastered on my face. Back in my room, I sat on my bed and stared at the wall. The wall that divided my brother and me. I imagined him there, falling into a deep sleep – his breath rattling, his chest struggling. I pictured his muscles, tight and restricted, his heart fighting each beat.

He was a boy whose body could never rest.

What I would give to take his pain away.

What I would do to make everything different.

But I couldn't do anything.

Instinctively, I picked up my phone and called Martha. She was the one who could make me feel better when things like this happened. She would talk about something completely irrelevant and funny and take my mind off it all for a bit. Weirdly, it went on to answerphone. That wasn't like her – usually she had her mobile on *all the time*. I left a quick voicemail asking her to call me.

I really needed a chat – this was the first time Martha hadn't been there for me. I stared at the phone resting uselessly in my hand and suddenly felt very alone.

Downstairs I could still hear Mum's voice and the slightly softer murmur of Dad's replies. Only a few weeks until Christmas. Usually I'd be excited, but this time I was dreading it – it's not like I could give anyone what they really wanted.

There was nothing I could do to help. I was useless.

MARTY

Mum had the film on again. She had already watched it twice yesterday. I knew it was her favourite, but this was taking obsession to the extreme. I walked in after another lousy day at school and could hear the familiar sounds reverberating through the flat. The same voices, the same music. I swear I'm going to have *Back to the Future* running through my brain for my entire life.

She didn't look up as I walked in. I slammed my bag against the sofa, but her eyes didn't leave the screen.

"Good day," she said, not so much a question as two words spoken together.

"Not really. I'm behind in English so I haven't got a clue what they're going on about and that makes me look thick, as always. I answered back in French and got sent out, and I had PE, which was crap."

"Cool. . ." Her hand fluttered in the air in a "quiet down" signal. "Look, it's the best bit! Watch it with me, Marty. It's so good."

I knew the bit she was talking about and I didn't need to see Marty McFly speed back through time in a lightning storm. I was sick of it. I was sick of all of it.

"You watched this last night," I said.

She leant forward. "Ssshh! It's important – there are messages in this – in all of this. I don't know why I didn't see it before."

I could see now that there was a notepad resting on her knee. She had been making notes. The writing was scrawled and difficult to make out.

"What messages, Mum?"

"So many, you wouldn't believe." She finally turned to me, her eyes wide and glazed-looking. "They're telling us there is danger. That there is always one man who can destroy our world –

look. . ." She prodded at her pad with her pen. "I've written it all down. We have to seek out the devil. Put the devil in our past, otherwise he'll destroy our future. It's the only way."

I seriously felt sick – like I could puke any moment. This was wrong. So wrong.

"Mum, please just turn this off. You need sleep – you need to rest. You're tired."

I picked up the remote and flicked the screen off. Surprisingly, Mum barely reacted. Instead she started writing down more things in her pad. "It's OK, I've seen enough," she said. "You can help me, Marty. We can work together to make things better. Will you help me?"

"Of course I will, Mum. I'll always help you."

She turned to face me, looking so happy – it was as if I'd just handed her the best present ever. For a moment she looked like her old self again.

"Good, because we need to get rid of J. I'm sure he's come to harm us."

Get rid of J? This was getting too weird.

"You don't mean that, Mum. You're tired. You need sleep."

She went to bed reluctantly, muttering under her breath. Who was I kidding – she probably wouldn't even go to sleep. I kept thinking I could hear her moving around in her room, but I couldn't bring myself to check.

Instead, I sat holding the card for social services, looking at the number printed neatly on it. Did she need help? Did *I* need help?

I thought of Dad and I could almost hear him in my head.

"She'll get better, Son; she just needs time. And us. No one else."

I put the card away again.

Mum was up and about when I got out of bed. Back on the computer, her notebook still out. She was wearing her pyjamas and hadn't bothered to brush her hair – it was lying in flat, knotted clumps around her face. When I was a kid she used to spend ages brushing her hair and making it look nice. For a moment my mind wandered and I found myself thinking about Daisy and how her hair seemed so soft and curly.

Daisy. Something in me stirred. I was meeting her tomorrow after school. This was a big deal – she was the first person who actually seemed to want to spend any time with me. I couldn't screw this up. Not this. Surely *something* in my life had to go OK.

Mum snorted loudly and started banging away at the keyboard, obviously typing out another angry message. This couldn't be good for her. I walked over to see what site she was on, but she quickly shifted in her seat so that I couldn't see the screen properly.

"Have you eaten?" I asked. I'm not even sure why I bothered. Her eyes were fixed to the screen, a tiny smile resting on her face.

"Yes of course," she said, but I knew she was lying. I'd already looked in the kitchen and there was still barely anything *to* eat. We needed to go shopping. We needed *money*. I knew she'd get her benefit money soon.

"Mum, have you got any cash on you? We need some bread and stuff."

"I'll go out later," she said. "Just eat what's there, I'm busy right now."

There were some cornflakes in the cupboard so

I ate them dry, convincing myself that they didn't taste too bad. Mum's purse sat on the kitchen side. I picked it up and had a quick peek inside. There was nothing really, just loose change and some receipts. I tipped out some coins, though. It was enough to get some bread and milk on the way home. Luckily, J had given me a fiver before he'd left, which I'd put on my lunch card. Thank God I'd be able to eat at school.

School.

I sighed and grabbed my bag, glancing over at Mum again. She'd gone back to typing furiously. However bad school felt, it was better than here.

Anywhere was better than here.

Mr Terry walked into my form room as I was just leaving. I guess I'd been expecting him, so it came as no surprise.

"You OK to come with me?" he asked quietly.

The two social workers were waiting in his office. Jenny and Debbie. Still fake-smiling. Still looking at me like I was some kid from primary school that needed help wiping his butt.

"Hi, Marty," Jenny said softly. "We just came to see how things were. How's your mum been?"

Don't tell them. Give her a chance to sort herself out...

"Fine. She's much better." The lies tripped off my tongue easily.

"Really?" Jenny was still smiling, her red lips almost too large for her face. Beside her Debbie was writing notes, her eyes never actually making contact with mine. Mr Terry stood next to me. I guess he was there to help make me feel better and, weirdly, he did. I liked having him there.

Jenny carried on. "I'm having trouble contacting her at the moment..."

"She's been busy. She's been – uh – sorting out the house. And writing. She's been writing on the computer. It's making her happy."

Well, that wasn't a complete lie, was it? Not really.

"That's good," Jenny nodded. She turned to Debbie. "We'll pop over and see Jo soon, have a quick catch up."

"She's honestly fine," I said, probably too quickly.

"It's nothing to worry about Marty – it's just part of our assessment. We can see you at school and your mum at home, and if everything's OK ... well, we can move on from there."

I nodded. That sounded hopeful. Maybe Mum *would* be all right when they visited. She was a bit hyped up at the moment, but she'd calm it down for them, surely.

"And school? How has Marty been here?"

Mr Terry coughed softly. "We had him leaving early the other day, unauthorized."

"I felt sick," I muttered.

"I see," said Jenny.

I frowned. This was so pointless – such a waste of time. They wanted me in school, then they dragged me into meetings like this!

"Can I go?" I asked, making a move towards the door.

"Of course. I only wanted to check that there's nothing wrong. Nothing at all that you're worried about." Jenny was looking intently now, and her words felt forceful. "We are here to help you, Marty. I promise that is all we want to do."

I hesitated, my hand resting on the door. Slowly, I shook my head.

Jenny stood up and walked over. "Remember, you have my details. You can call me if anything changes."

"I'm fine," I said. "We both are, seriously."

But as I left the room, there was a little voice in my head: *tell them the truth.*

Mum isn't sleeping.

Mum isn't eating.

Mum's cracking up.

I think I might be, too.

DAISY

Harry woke me up with his coughing. He'd been making noises for most of the night, and I heard Mum and Dad moving around in his room. At around six a.m. he started coughing really badly. There was no way I could sleep after that.

I had a quick shower instead, letting the steady stream of water wake me up properly. Wrapping a towel around me, I walked back into my bedroom soundlessly. I didn't want to bother anyone. I could still hear Mum in Harry's room, talking to him softly. I wondered how long she'd been there and whether she'd slept at all last night.

I lay down on my bed and read through some

stuff on my phone. It wasn't really that interesting. Martha hadn't uploaded much – just one cutesy picture of her and Flynn. Strangely, there were very few comments about it this time – maybe her and Cara had sorted things out. I'd tried calling her again last night, but she hadn't picked up. A few hours later she'd messaged me, saying she gone out with Flynn and his mates. It's not like I minded – it was fine. But I really missed talking to her. She always made me feel better.

I flicked through pictures, memes and stupid comments. Without really thinking about it, I found myself typing out Marty's name in the search button. I wanted to see what his profile looked like. But I couldn't find anything – he didn't seem to be on it.

Just like at school, he was invisible.

In just a few hours' time I was meeting this guy and I knew nothing about him, except for some scary rumours and negative comments from other people. I was meeting up with someone who seemed to barely exist in our world.

Maybe I should have been worried, but I wasn't.

Martha was waiting in the form room when I walked in. She was already chatting to one of Cara's close mates, Stacey, and they were laughing, so I assumed things were fine between them all now.

I walked over, throwing my bag on the desk. "All right?"

Martha looked up. "All right, Daisy? Stacey was just filling me in on last night's party. Apparently Cara hooked up with that sixth former, Jamel?"

"Party?" I looked at them blankly. "What party?"

Martha at least had the decency to look a bit sheepish. "Well, it wasn't so much a party. More a gathering – you know. Flynn's mate Gavin arranged it. It was kind of last-minute, Flynn just took me along."

Stacey laughed. "It was sooo funny. Those guys are pretty crazy."

"So you lot all went, then?" I said, glaring at Stacey.

"Well, Cara went, obviously. What party *doesn't* she go to? And a few of us went with her," Stacey said.

"At least me and Cara sorted things out. She's

happy I'm with Flynn now — she's moved on." Martha was making out it was no big deal, but she'd never left me out of stuff before.

I sat down, feeling properly grumpy. "Cool."

"Anyway, since when would your mum let you go to a party mid-week?"

"She might have," I said, even though I knew that wasn't true. "She's so distracted now, I doubt she'd even notice I was gone."

Martha moved in her chair so she was facing me properly. "Look, I'm sorry I didn't call you, OK? I just didn't think it would be your sort of thing."

"What do you mean?"

"Well — you know. I get it that things are pretty hard for you right now. But, Daisy ... you can be pretty heavy sometimes. It's nice just have a night where we don't have to be serious."

"Oh, I'm sorry, I didn't know I brought you down." My words were like ice. It felt like each one was cutting at my throat.

"It's not that, Daisy. I didn't mean that." Her eyes flicked away from me. "You know it does us good to be around other people for a while."

"Yeah," I said. "Maybe it does."

I turned away. I didn't want her to see my face. I didn't want her to see how much she'd hurt me.

School seemed to drag, and I spent most of it in a moody haze. But I was relieved I wasn't walking home with Martha. She was probably right; we did spend a lot of time together. And why was she saying I brought her down? This was the girl who spent most of her time obsessing over her soppy, dim-witted, so-called boyfriend.

She needed to get a grip.

I wasn't in the best of moods meeting Marty, but I was seriously pleased to see him. He was waiting at the gate as I walked over, as tatty-looking as always. His stupid big coat made him look almost crow-like and his hair was sticking up in all directions. But when he smiled, I could feel the stress of the day melt away.

"You look pissed off," he said. "Was your day really that bad?"

"Worse. Where are we going, anyway?"

"Dunno. Shall we just head into town? I fancy a milkshake or something."

I raised an eyebrow. "A milkshake? In this weather?" He grinned at me.

"Milkshake it is," I said.

We started walking out of the main gates and a strange silence settled over us. It was a little weird, but I wasn't sure what I should talk about. The group? School? Why were we even meeting up anyway?

"I lasted the day, you might be pleased to know," he said at last. "I can't say it was the most thrilling experience, but it'll get a lot of people off my back."

"Like who? Your mum?"

"I guess ... And Mr Terry and a few other people. They don't tend to like it if you miss school, funnily enough. Make it into a big deal."

"Well, it kind of is," I said, immediately feeling like some kind of lame swot. "I mean, I get it that you don't like the place – I don't either half the time. But it's kind of important unless you want to end up a total waster."

"Bit harsh," he said, smiling. "But I get your point. Are you related to Mr Terry?"

"Ha! No, but I like him. He's all right."

"Yeah – I guess he is."

We were walking down the main road now on the route into town. Marty walked fast – I guess because of those long legs of his. I found myself having to keep up.

"So why was your day so bad?" he asked.

I thought of Martha and her barbed comments earlier. Even the memory of it made me feel a little sick.

"Honestly, it's nothing," I said. "But put it this way, I was glad to get out of there today."

We ended up at the small ice-cream parlour on the main square. This place was one of Harry's favourites – painted brightly inside and out, with a view of the large water fountain outside. I pointed out the seats by the window so me and Marty could look out at it. The whole square looked so pretty at dusk, all lit up with twinkly bright lights and decorations. In the distance I could hear a brass band playing Christmas carols, and – despite myself – a warm feeling spread over me. I sipped at my strawberry milkshake.

"It's so lovely out there," I said. "I love how winter means the evenings get darker quicker – it makes everything more peaceful and beautiful."

Marty nodded. "I love night-time. I'm definitely a night owl."

"And it's so Christmassy now – just look at it all," I sighed. "I keep forgetting how close Christmas is."

I saw Marty's face darken a little and wished I hadn't said anything.

"I doubt we'll do much," he said, taking a sip of his drink. "It's not like we have a big family or anything. Last year it was basically just me and Mum – Mum's boyfriend J went to the pub for most of it. It wouldn't be so bad if we went to my Auntie Jackie's – she keeps asking us over."

"Is that who runs your stall – your auntie?"

"Yeah, she's my dad's sister. My mum says she's interfering, but I think it's just because she reminds her too much of. . ."

Marty's voice broke and he looked down, shaking his head a little. "It's just annoying, that's all. Jackie really helps me and I know she wants to do more."

He sighed. "How can I give Mum a decent Christmas? It's not like I can give her anything she wants."

"Like what?"

"Like ... I dunno, *anything*. I haven't even thought about a Christmas present for her, to be honest. It's like the other day, I was walking past the bookshop and all I wanted to do was buy her this book she's always loved..." He laughed, but what came out was a dry, sad-sounding noise. "She had a copy once, but it got, well, destroyed. Anyway, that's something I want to do – something small that would make her smile – but I can't."

I found myself reaching over and gently touching his hand. "It's lovely that you wanted to, though." He didn't move away, but his head was still dipped. "What book was it, anyway?"

"*Watership Down*," he muttered. "It's some lame book about bloody rabbits."

I giggled. "It's more than that – it's amazing! You should read it sometime."

He looked at me. "Maybe..." With his head lifted, I could properly see his eyes. They were so warm and brown with sparks of yellow, reminding me of fire.

"But enough of me whinging on – you mentioned Harry. Is that your brother? He must be cool."

A rush of pride swept over me. "He is. *So* cool. And so brave."

"Brave?"

". . . He has this condition, it makes his muscles progressively weaker. He's often in a lot of pain." I sighed. "It's pretty shit, actually."

"That's awful. Really awful. I'm so sorry."

His words didn't sound fake. Or wrong. Or stupid. They sounded sincere and honest and I needed to hear it.

Then he took both my hands in his and we just sat there for a while, holding hands and looking out at the glittering lights that brightened up the dark world outside us.

MARTY

I offered to walk her home. It had been nice at the ice-cream place – something different. It was surprisingly easy to talk to Daisy and I found myself chatting to her about all sorts of crap but that didn't matter. Within two hours we knew the names of our first pets, favourite TV shows and preferred flavour of Slush Puppy.

It was good. Great, in fact. And it was pretty late by the time we started walking back. Town was properly dark and Daisy giggled like a kid as we walked down the high street where the market would be set up later. She stood under the huge Christmas tree, her eyes almost sparkling brighter than the hundreds of fairy lights dotted in its branches.

"I always loved Christmas," she said softly, her face still tipped up. The light glowed against her skin, making it seem more delicate than ever. "I always loved it so much. But now ... now it's just like a countdown. Every time I wonder if this will be Harry's last one."

"I guess it just about making each one special – magical. Living in the now."

I grimaced slightly. My answer seemed so lame. But she turned to me. "And you do that? You live in the now?"

"I remember my dad once telling me that the only thing no one can guarantee is their tomorrow. So you just have to live for now. It was just something he said. I didn't say I followed it... But I dunno ... maybe I should."

We started walking. She was so close I could feel the breeze of her arm as she moved, and part of me wanted to take her hand again, but I felt too shy. Too awkward. How did I know if she wanted that? She might think I was a total creep.

"You *should* follow it," she said. "It's good advice. Do you think you spend a lot of time in the past?"

"Maybe. . ." I wasn't so sure I wanted to get into this.

"I mean. . ." I could feel her hesitate, and her pace slowed. "I know it must be hard, your dad dying, I get that. But everything since? You getting excluded from Greenfields, beating up that boy? It seems like you're stuck in this role now – with this bad-boy image. But I don't think that's really you."

"You don't?" I couldn't help grinning. "I'm disappointed. I've been working on that for ages."

"Yeah, well. That's kind of the point. I think you enjoy this stupid reputation you have. It gives you an excuse not to do what you should be doing. It stops you moving forward."

"Moving forward? To what?" I knew my voice was hardening, but I couldn't help it – without even realizing, she was picking at old wounds. "What do I move forward *to*, Daisy? College? University? I can't leave Mum. I need to be out earning, for both of us."

"You might need to put yourself first for once."

I shook my head and we kept walking. The gap between us had increased. I didn't like that – I didn't want the evening to end that way.

"It's cool you saying that, but I'm fine. I just need to do what I have to do."

We carried on walking, but Daisy's pace had slowed a little. I glanced over at her. A small frown was pressed into her face.

"Did you really beat up that boy?" she asked suddenly. "The one at your last school."

I half laughed. "Kwaime. What do you think? Half the school thinks I beat him unconscious. The other half thinks I actually killed him."

I sighed. "The truth is, he was a mate. A good mate. But all of a sudden he got an attitude, started hanging around with this older guy, Tyler Walker, and wanted to show everyone that he was hard. The two of them came at me one break-time, started giving me grief – said stuff about my mum—"

"That's out of order," she said.

Out of order. That's putting it mildly.

"Mum had been pretty bad then. Dad's death had tipped her over the edge, and she spent days on end in her pyjamas, not even washing. Kwaime was one of the few people who I still had back at the flat. I thought he was all right. He understood. But what was it he called her again? Oh yeah – a piss-stained pill-head. A nutter."

The memory still stung. This was why I didn't let anyone near the flat now. Daisy was quiet, letting me fill the air with my words.

"So, yeah, I hit him. And he kept saying stuff, and I hit him again. Before it kicked off, Tyler had been telling him to 'get me' but as soon as I was on Kwaime, Tyler legged it. Anyway, at one point Kwaime came at me and we kind of fell into each other. He caught his head on the bench and was out cold."

I still remember it. The blood. Kwaime rolling on to the floor. The grunting sound coming from his mouth. He sounded like an animal. He was my mate. We used to kick a ball around – we used to have a laugh. But then he was lying in a pool of blood and I hadn't cared. Not in that moment. Not at all.

Daisy's voice snapped my mind back to the present. "Oh God, that's awful. Was he ... was he OK?"

"He had concussion and a bad cut on his head. But none of it was as bad as they thought at first. That didn't matter, though – it was enough. Tyler told them I'd attacked Kwaime for no reason. There weren't any other witnesses..."

"And they excluded you for that?"

"It was a managed move, really. The final straw. But it might as well have been an exclusion. They wanted me out. They'd had enough. I'd gone too far."

How does anyone come back from that?

Daisy chatted the whole way back. Hearing about the fight hadn't seemed to put her off me, weirdly. If anything, she seemed more natural and relaxed. I loved it when she laughed and her tiny nose wrinkled up. She had been telling me about Martha.

"I have such annoying friends," she was saying. First she had started out all stressed and angry about it, but now she was proper laughing.

"You can bet she'll be messaging me tomorrow. Telling me she's sorry for being a cow and please can I help her decide what to wear for her date with Flynn, because he might dump her if she wore the wrong shade of blue."

I smiled. "And that'd be all right? If she messaged you?"

"Yeah, course." Daisy stopped walking and turned to face me. "She's a good mate usually, but she doesn't always get why I'm so intense. Why should she? A big deal for Martha is whether her parents will let her out that night. She doesn't know what it's like to be me."

We continued to walk. The silence felt natural. Being here with Daisy felt natural. I liked it. I liked the fact that I could just be *me* with her.

That was good.

I guess it was because we were quite similar, really. We spent too much time dealing with someone else's problems, trying to convince ourselves that it was OK when some days it really wasn't.

"Do you worry about Harry all the time?" I asked. "I do with my mum, so I guess it's the same for you."

"I suppose..." Her voice wandered off a little.

"I do worry about Harry a lot, but it's weird – I worry about other stuff too. Like something bad happening to Mum or Dad . . . or me. I feel like so much is out of our control. And everything could go wrong. I don't know. . ."

She was shaking her head.

"What?"

"I just don't normally talk about this stuff. It's easier not to."

I snorted. "Jesus, I'm always going on about it. I just can't stand people telling me what I already know."

"It's good you can do that."

I shrugged. "I've never really thought about it before. I guess me and Dad used to talk a lot, you know? Even if it was just a bit of banter. But it helped because I could tell him about stuff that was bugging me. I had to get it off my chest, otherwise I'd just explode."

"He sounds like a great guy."

"He was." I kick a stone into the road, distracted now. "It's not so easy now he's not here. I still talk to him sometimes, though. In my head. Does that sound mad?"

Daisy stopped walking. "No. Not at all."

"I guess what I'm trying to say is that I get it. I get what it's like to be worried about someone all the time. It's hard. Not everyone understands that." I paused. "Sometimes you *do* need to talk about it."

Daisy nodded. "Maybe I do. And maybe this has helped a bit – tonight. I've enjoyed it."

"I've enjoyed it too."

We stopped on one of the main avenues that ran through the back of town and I looked down the street behind Daisy. Mum always used to call this "Money Side". The houses were big, with massive front gardens and garages.

"You live *here?*" I asked, trying to keep the surprise out of my voice.

Daisy gestured. "Yeah, that one. The tattiest one on the street, but it's ours. I think me and Martha are the only ones who live this far across town – it's probably why we ended up being mates."

"You should've gone to Greenfields, it's only down the road."

Daisy laughed. "I told you! My dad is an old-school socialist – he wanted me to go to the same comp he did. I didn't mind, most of my primary school mates went to St David's, anyway."

Her parents had to be doing all right for themselves. It was dead expensive here.

"When we moved here, both of my parents were working in IT," she said, reading my mind. "Things are different now that Mum looks after Harry full-time. Anyway, we'll have to move soon."

"Why? It's so decent here."

"We need somewhere bigger but cheaper. Harry needs a bedroom downstairs and a wet room... He's already struggling to get up and down stairs." She smiled, but it seemed false somehow. "It's OK, a move will be exciting."

"Maybe you'll move to the poor side of town with me?"

"That wouldn't be so bad." Her smile was brighter this time.

We stood there for what felt like for ever. I could feel nerves jumping around under my skin like tiny prickles of electricity. I wanted to take her hands again and pull her towards me. She was looking straight at me, a tiny smile resting on her lips.

Those lips, though.

"I guess I better go. . ." she said, taking a step backwards. Her eyes still locked on mine.

"Yeah, I guess you better."

Stupid answer. Why wasn't I thinking properly?

"I'll see you soon then?"

"Yeah . . . I'll message you? We can do something again?"

"I could see you after school tomorrow? Maybe just for a bit?" She sounded shy. Why did I like that so much?

Yes. Get in.

"Yeah – why not."

She grinned. "OK, see you then."

I could feel myself inwardly groan as she went to move away. That was a chance. I should've at least flirted a bit more.

She liked me, didn't she? Otherwise she wouldn't even be here.

"Daisy!"

Jesus, what was I doing?

She turned straight away, the hint of a smile still on her lips.

"Thanks again. I mean ... I really enjoyed myself."

Oh my God, I'm dying.

"Me too," she said. "You really are a man of mystery."

I let her go then, and watched her as she walked towards her house. What did she think of me? What would it be like when we saw each other tomorrow? The only thing I knew for sure was that this girl had got under my skin. In a good way.

In a really good way.

Whatever was going on between me and Daisy, I wanted it to keep going. And I wanted that good feeling – that nice vibe – to stay with me for the rest of my day. But that was never going to happen. To be fair, back at home, things didn't start off too bad. I heated up some soup for me and Mum and she even ate it. But she was still talking nonsense, and she still hadn't bothered to comb her hair. She looked a mess.

She was in an excited mood, telling me more about the people she'd been chatting to online.

"Everything they tell us is lies," she said as she spooned the red-hot soup into her mouth.

"Jesus, Mum!" I snatched the spoon from her hand, but she was oblivious.

"The news, the TV programmes they fill our heads with, the films... They're trying to numb us, make us brain dead – but the messages are all there if you're clever enough to pick them up."

"Did you go out today?" I asked her bluntly.

"Of course, I went for a walk. I got lots of fresh air – it's good for the brain," she said, tapping the side of her head frantically. I don't know why she was even bothering to lie; I could see she was still in the same pyjamas she'd been in that morning. They seemed to be welded to her skin.

"Those women came over again," she said. "You know, from the social. I know their game, of course. I know who're they're *really* working for ... but I have to let them get on with it. Answer their questions and they'll soon go away."

I looked at her, confused. "They work for the council, Mum."

"Oh, Marty," she sighed. "You're so naive. Of

course they don't work for the council. They're *spies*. They watch the people who know too much." She prodded a finger at her chest. "I know too much, you see, so I'm a risk. They have to keep a close eye on me."

"Oh-kay..." I let the word hang in the air.

"But I'm too wise for all that!" she laughed – a raspy, reedy sound that seemed to come deep from her chest. "I didn't let them in. Just spoke to them through the crack of the door – told them I had a bug and needed to rest. I couldn't have them in here, seeing my notes – looking at my computer."

There were two new A4 pads on the dining room table behind Mum. She'd already filled one up. I'd looked inside it earlier, but all I could see was incomprehensible scrawl.

"They'll be back, though," she sighed. "They said as much. We need to get rid of them, Marty. But how? I need to think."

"Maybe they just want to help?"

I couldn't quite believe I was saying it, but the words just fell out of my mouth.

"*Help?* Are you crazy? They're not here to *help*. They're here to *contain me*."

I looked at her hopelessly – her eyes wild, her hair matted and greasy, her mouth continuing to move as she muttered complaints under her breath. This was worse than she'd ever been. I didn't even recognize her – how the hell was this my mum?

My *mum*.

Would she get better once J was back? Would he help her, or would he just hide away down the pub? He wasn't the best, but at least he was someone to talk to.

"At least J will be home soon," I said, more to myself than her.

"*J?*" Mum almost screeched his name. Her eyes looked even wider. "J? Are you serious?"

She carried on staring at me, waiting for me to say something, but I didn't reply. What could I say? Before I knew what was going on, Mum's soup went flying. She'd thrown it across the table. There was soup everywhere.

"J is *behind all of this*," she hissed, pushing her

face close to mine. "We can't trust him. He's a plant. He's spying on us."

"Mum..." I started, but words completely failed me. She was acting crazy and I was bricking it. Her eyes. Her words. It was too much. This was all too much.

"I will be getting rid of J," she said, her words like ice splinters in my ear. "He is the *devil*. He needs to *go*."

DAISY

So I went home with the cheesiest grin on my face, I couldn't help it. There was just something about Marty that made me smile – which was pretty ironic, considering he wasn't the happiest guy I'd ever met. But the truth was, being with him felt real. For once, I could be totally myself, not pretend I was someone else.

The daughter who got on with things without complaining.

The girl who didn't act up at school.

The friend who listened and knew her place.

Marty made me feel like it was OK to talk about Harry – like I wasn't going to totally do his head in with it, or anything. Marty understood because he was going through similar stuff. I thought of him, alone in the flat with his mum. I had my parents, my grandparents, my friends – other people around me. Marty was alone. That must really hurt sometimes.

And he didn't hurt that kid deliberately. He lets everyone think he did because it's easier that way. It's easier to keep people away than it is to have them close.

I got that. I really did.

And it didn't bother me at all.

As I walked back into the house, I felt the usual tension shift on to me – but it wasn't as bad as it usually was. Maybe just being out with someone different had helped? It was quiet inside, just the soft hum of the TV and sounds of the dishwasher in the kitchen. Mum was dozing on the sofa and Dad was working in the dining room.

"Good time?" he asked, walking over to me and pulling me into a hug. "I've saved you some dinner in the microwave."

"Thanks," I said, shrugging off my coat. "And yeah – I had a nice time."

We both looked at Mum, sleeping on her side. She looked so peaceful, almost child-like with her soft, delicate features. When she was resting, I couldn't see the frown lines or the dark circles under her eyes. I loved how Dad had draped one of our old blankets around her to keep her warm.

"Harry has been hard work today," Dad said. "His cold has come back with force, so his lungs are really struggling. Your mum had to pick up a new inhaler today, and he already hates it. She's worried that he'll get worse if he doesn't take it. I keep telling her—"

"I know you do."

He didn't need to say it. We were always telling her to stop worrying. To stop fearing the worst. Everything would be all right. But we knew the words sounded hollow. We knew we were practically lying. The worst *would* happen one day.

We were just waiting.

"She's so tired," I said.

She's always tired.

"We'll get through it," Dad whispered in my ear. "I'm working on her. I'm helping her see that she needs to let go a little – let other people help. But she feels guilty all the time, that's the trouble. She thinks she owes it to Harry to be the one to care for him all the time."

"I don't get why she feels so guilty. It's not her fault – it's not anyone's fault."

I felt Dad's arms loosen quickly, and he pulled away, frowning.

"She hasn't told you yet. She promised me she would tell you."

Oh God.

"Tell me what?"

More bad news? How could there be more?

My stomach twisted, the knots in it tightening further.

Dad took my arm and led me into the kitchen, carefully closing the door behind us. I wondered what food was waiting for me. I didn't even know if I was still hungry.

"We always knew that Harry's condition is genetic..." Dad's voice seemed far-off. I couldn't stop thinking about food – why was I thinking about food? I stared dumbly at the wall while he talked.

"But when we were tested, we found out. . . Well, we found out that your mum carries the gene. *That's* why she feels so guilty. She feels like she's given this – this awful thing – to Harry."

Genetic? I shook my head, as if I could make the words I'd just heard fall out of my head. I'd never thought of Harry's condition like that before – I didn't know much about that sort of stuff. We'd covered it a bit in science – the fact that our parents passed their eye colours on to us, or hair, or whatever. But I'd never considered the bad stuff. That a parent could "give" an illness to their child – something that could make them weak and leave them in pain. Something that could kill them.

Dad took my hand in his and squeezed it, making me look at him again. He was crying. It always felt weird to see him crying – my big, tall dad with his crazy haircut, tattoos and loud mouth. But so often now his words were replaced with tears.

"The gene is only carried in girls, Daisy," he said. And I didn't understand what he meant at first. I just carried on staring at him. "You can be tested too," he said patiently. "Once you're sixteen. If you want to."

His words carved through my belly like fire. Suddenly everything felt fuzzy, unreal – like I wasn't in the room any more. I had to take a breath, trying desperately to root myself back in the moment and make sense of what he'd just told me.

I could be carrying this? If I have a child, I could make them sick like Harry?

This could happen again and again.

The nightmare may never be over.

Mum was waiting for me in the kitchen when I got up the next morning. Harry was sat in the living room, looking content with his toast and kids' TV.

"Dad spoke to you," she said straight away.

I looked up at her red-rimmed eyes, at her swallow cheeks and dry lips. She seemed to be disappearing in front of me.

"Yes," I said carefully. "He told me about the genetic thing."

She was still looking at me. Waiting for a reaction. Wanting me to say more.

What, Mum? Do you really want to know the truth? That I cry myself to sleep most nights. That I'm miserable too. That I'm not sure if I want to be tested, because I couldn't bear to know if I was carrying this awful, twisted gene inside me. That I'd rather not know.

But you don't want to know the truth, do you?

You don't want to know how scared I am, because you already feel bad.

You don't want to know how angry I am because you're struggling and I can't make you any more stressed.

You don't want to know how confused I feel, because you haven't got time to listen to my pathetic worries.

And you don't want to know that as of this moment I never want to be a mum, because I can't end up like you.

I won't.

I pushed out a breath, realizing I'd been holding it. I felt the numbness spread over me. It was oddly reassuring.

"It's fine, Mum. Honestly. I'll deal with it."

She paused. "You can get tested, next year ... If you want?" she said gently.

I started making my breakfast. I didn't want to think about this. Instead I thought about Marty. Of the "goodnight" text he'd sent me before I'd drifted off to sleep and the "good morning" message that had woken me up. Thinking about Marty made things a little easier.

"Daisy?" Mum said hesitantly. "I've been talking to your dad."

I sat down with my bowl of cereal, staring at her blankly. What now? Was there another genetic illness they wanted to tell me about? Something else that would ruin my life?

Mum half smiled. "I've agreed to contact carers support. And the council. I'm looking at getting some respite." She was talking softly now, looking at me like she meant it. "I need to let go a little, I see that now. I'm tired. And Harry would benefit from going to some groups and being around other children. I'll have time for myself." She reached for my hand. "And I'll have time for you."

My breakfast caught in my throat. I almost

choked and had to swallow hard. I took another gulp. This wasn't what I was expecting. "Mum, I—"

"It's consuming. *All of this*. But we are a family. We need each other. And I want to be here for you like you've been for us."

I felt the tears pooling in my eyes and nodded, trying to blink them away.

She smiled.

"I'm sorry I've been so ... well, distant." Her voice broke slightly. "I don't know how life is going to turn out. It makes me so protective of Harry. I can't face what might happen."

I thought of Marty again. Of the things he said yesterday, the words that had made so much sense.

"The only thing no one can guarantee is their tomorrow," I said.

Mum looked at me and blinked, the tears spilling from her eyes. "That's so true," she said. "And that's why we need to make sure we enjoy every moment of our 'today'."

*

I got to my form room early and sat at my desk straight away, focusing on my book to drown out the noise of the room. Martha was late in, as usual.

"Look, I'm sorry about yesterday," she said, slumping down next to me. "I was a bit harsh."

I could've gone into a lengthy rant about how she'd upset me. How she'd made me feel like I just annoy her now, and got in the way. But what would be the point? She wouldn't listen – she'd probably get more stressed.

I sighed. "It's OK."

It wasn't OK, though. Not really. But neither of us wanted to acknowledge that.

"How's Harry?"

Her automatic question.

It dawned on me that she asked this every day. But how much did she actually care? She hadn't visited Harry in *months*.

"He's great," I said, my words dripping with sarcasm. "Coughing all night, crying with pain all day – and he'll probably need a wheelchair soon."

"Oh."

Martha was chewing her lip and picking at her nails – something she always did when she felt awkward or didn't know what to say – and I suddenly felt bad. None of this was her fault; she was just caught up in the edges of my world. So what if she got it wrong sometimes? She was still my mate.

I shrugged at her. "Anyway, what's the latest with you?"

I watched as she visibly relaxed in front of me, uncurling like a cat and telling me all about her wonderful evening with Flynn. I tried to look interested.

I decided to go out at lunchtime. It was easy enough to do – I just told reception that I needed to pick my PE kit up from home and they believed me. One benefit that comes from being a good girl – no one questions you.

Some year elevens were already hanging around outside school when I left, and my eyes drifted through the throngs looking for Marty but I couldn't see him.

Luckily most of them went in the opposite direction, towards the shops at the end of the road, where the chippie and newsagent were. I wondered where Marty was. I never saw him in the hall at lunch. I half expected him to have his own hideaway somewhere, or some sort of arrangement where he could leave a few minutes early. Marty seemed to follow his own rules. It was like he didn't belong with the rest of the school.

He'd sent me a text earlier. One that had lifted my mood and pasted a cheesy grin on my face.

Can't wait to see you later, sunshine girl.

Sunshine girl. No one had ever called me that before. I wasn't even sure it was a name that suited me. How could I be a sunshine girl? But I wasn't complaining. I kind of liked it.

It wasn't a long walk to the shop. The day had turned bright and crisp – the perfect weather for clearing my head and escaping the noise of school. As I walked, I glanced at the houses I passed by – most of the ones on my right were large Victorian terraces, most of them with Christmas decorations up. Even though the decorations were turned off, I could still see the shadows of festivity there, in the hanging lights and faded signs. My mum had always liked these types of houses, and wanted to live in one. I remember when I was little, we went to look at one once. It was a few streets away from this road, and was huge, with an attic room and cellar. It had looked amazing, like I could've explored it for ever.

But then Harry was born and everything changed.

The other side of street was a different picture. It wasn't quite as pretty, with mainly industrial units and tatty shops that had closed down ages ago. Then there was the main road that snaked into the Yeovil Estate. I knew this was where Marty's flat was – in fact, I could see the corner of it poking up behind the trees. I wondered what it was like living so high up, with a view over the whole town.

Would you feel like a bird trapped in a cage?

I got to the bookshop five minutes later, my

hands now numb with cold and my face tingling. I found what I was looking for quickly and took it to the counter. The bookseller smiled as she rang it through the till.

"*Watership Down*," she said. "Great choice. Is it for you?"

"No," I replied. "It's for a friend."

I was hoping it would make him smile.

MARTY

Daisy messaged me – I got it while I was sat at the back of the art block, trying to get away from everyone. I hated lunchtime the most. This was when people were at their loudest and most irritating – standing in the quad throwing food at each other, and generally acting like mugs. To be fair, it was mainly the lower years. Most of my year had sloped off down to the shops, but I couldn't face that either. I had no money to buy anything decent and nowhere else to go. It wasn't like I could hang around with anyone.

Hey, mate, fancy knocking around with me for a bit? Yeah, it's me, Marty. The headcase. The screw-

up. I promise not to kick your head in if you let me have a handful of crisps.

I couldn't quite see it working out, somehow.

If I went to the market, I wouldn't come back. I knew that. I'd end up staying with Jackie for the day, no matter how much she'd try and persuade me otherwise. That was just how it was. To avoid the temptation, I just had to stay away, for now at least.

Could I go home?

Yeah, right.

Home.

Jesus, even the thought of it twisted my guts. I wasn't sure I ever wanted to go back there. What would face me when I opened the door? Did I even care any more? A while ago, this was all I thought about. Mum – just praying she'd be OK. That she'd go back to being herself and that we'd make things work. But now it was different. Something else niggled at me.

Why do I have to be the strong one? I miss Dad too. I needed him just as much as she did.

My hand slapped the ground, and the rough

earth stung my skin. I didn't care. I slammed it again, harder.

I still need him. I need someone.

But I've got no one, and nowhere to go.

So I sat at the back of the art building like a loser, freezing my arse off, counting the number of ravens that swooped on to the field looking for food. I was feeling pretty miserable and wondering what the hell was the point of any of this. Why didn't I get up and go? Why didn't I just start walking and keep going until I was far away from here? I didn't have to face it again.

Then Daisy sent me a message.

**I got you a little something. Will give it
to you after school. Love Miss Sunshine.**

The smile escaped, I couldn't help it. I thought immediately of her eyes, her face – her soft words that seemed to make so much sense.

I thought of her and my mood lifted.

It didn't last, of course.

It all went to crap in the bogs – an irony not

lost on me. Most of the time I avoid being in those types of places – *communal* places. But I'd left home as fast as I could that morning and I needed a piss, so what choice did I have? It was nearly the end of lunch and I figured I would be OK – I wouldn't get any hassle. I should've known better.

I hadn't been there long before they walked in – Josh and his pathetic mates, Reece and Scott.

"Aw, look who it is! The hard nut," he sniggered at me.

I zipped up my flies and walked to the sink, ignoring him completely. I couldn't stand looking at his smug face. His goon Scott was even more irritating. He reminded me of a rat, both in size and his facial expressions. It was a wonder that no one had punched his massive teeth back into his mouth where they belonged. It might've done him a favour.

"Not talking to us, Marty?" said Reece. He was tall and thin with a whiny voice. He always sounded like he had a cold.

I dried my hand slowly under the dryer. "I'll talk if you want. But I don't think you'll want to hear what I have to say."

Josh laughed again. "What is it with you? You come into this school acting like you own the place, looking down at us all like we're pieces of scum beneath you? I don't get it. Haven't even seen you touch anyone. I think that rep of yours is crap – I don't think you could hurt anyone. I bet you're soft as, really."

For a second my mind flashed to an image of Kwaime, of the blood pouring from his mouth and nose. His face all ruined. So much blood – on me too. All over me.

"Believe what you want." I shrugged as I tried to move away – away from these idiots and their irritating faces. But Josh stood in front of me to block my way. He reached up and laid his hand on my shoulder and I instinctively knocked it off. I didn't want him touching me. I didn't want him anywhere near me. But he was in my space, and the rage I'd felt earlier was now boiling up like steam. My brain felt fuzzy and hot with it. I had to blink hard as I tried to regain control.

"Go on then. You're so bloody hard – take me on. One on one." Josh looked at me with his stupid, thick grin. "Prove you're hard, because we don't believe it. In fact. . ."

He leant in close now, and I could smell his breath. It stank. I jolted back.

". . .I reckon you're a pussy. I reckon you beat up some small kid and now you're making out you're something you're not."

He shoved me, but I kept my balance. I kept calm. I kept breathing. But the anger was rising.

There was so much pressure in my head. Too much pressure.

"Go on," he spat. "Prove it."

"You nutter," said Scott in the corner. "Absolute nutter."

I took a breath.

Kwaime. That word, the word he said. About my mum.

Blood. So much blood.

I shoved Josh away. "I'm not a nutter!" I shouted.

But he came closer again. "Yeah? Well we reckon you are."

In that instant, I moved so quickly. I wanted

to slam him against the wall. I wanted to ram my hand into his face. Break his nose. Take those words and force them down his throat. Fill his mouth with blood.

Make him fear me.

My fist flew up, but instead of hitting his face, I slammed it into the wall – hard. Blind pain rocketed me back.

"Just leave it!" I yelled.

And I walked. I walked right out of there. Tears were biting at my eyes, and blood was seeping out of my knuckles. I could hear them laughing behind me.

"See – bloody headcase."

But I'm not.

I'm not.

They don't get it. No one does.

"Leave it!" I shouted again, over my shoulder, moving faster now. My fist was throbbing as pain seared though my body. I started to run.

And I ran straight into Mr Terry.

"Hey! Not so fast!" He held my arm gently and drew me back. "Marty – what's going on?"

I felt wild, like an animal that needed to escape. I twisted out of his grasp.

"Get off me!" I carried on walking but he followed me, his footsteps echoing on the floor. A hollow sound. A drumbeat.

"Just go away," I hissed.

I'm not worth it.

"I'm not going anywhere, Marty. I can take you somewhere to calm down. But I'm not leaving you."

"I just want to go!" I yelled, my voice bouncing off the walls and making me sound more crazy than ever. I almost laughed. Isn't this what they wanted? They all wanted to see Marty lose his head. Well, here I am! I'm finally doing it. I could see faces pressed up against classroom doors, and looking over the balcony. They would all be whispering. They would all be spreading their nasty gossip about me.

But hey, what was new?

For one bleak second I wondered if Daisy was among them. I imagined her watching me.

No – don't do this. Don't act like they expect you to.

It felt like a thousand eyes were staring at me.

I swear I could still hear Josh laughing. But my body was heavy. My legs were lead. Mr Terry put his hand on my shoulder. It was a gentle touch and I immediately felt my body slump.

I wanted my dad.

Can you give me that, Mr Terry? Can you?

I was done running. Where else could I go? There was nowhere.

Nowhere.

I had to face it.

"Maybe we can go in here?" said Mr Terry, gesturing to an empty classroom.

I followed him in and stood there as he perched himself on a desk. I couldn't sit, my legs felt too restless. I couldn't look at him, either.

"What happened?" he asked. "Tell me. And I want the truth."

"I was in the toilets and they followed me in. . ." My words were sludge. "They started on me. I didn't touch them."

"*Who* started on you?"

"Josh and his lot."

"Josh in your year?"

I nodded. I didn't care that I was a grass. I was done caring.

"What did they say to you?"

"They were just trying to start something … making out I act all hard." I looked up then, faced him out. "I just keep myself to myself. Everyone here thinks I'm some tough guy, but it's just rumours. I'm not – I'm not anything."

I could see Mr Terry watching me closely, taking it all in.

"So they tried to fight you?"

"Yeah." I shrugged. "But I didn't touch them."

"Your fist took a pounding, though. What was it – a wall?"

"It's fine." I flexed it to slow him, trying not to flinch. The blood was drying now and the knuckles were stiff but it was clear I hadn't done too much damage – to myself or the wall.

"We'll get it checked out just to be sure," he said. "And I need to speak to Josh. This can't go on."

I shrugged. He could speak to Josh but that was unlikely to stop anything.

"You missed another day of school this week,"

he said. He sounded sad, like he was genuinely disappointed. I almost believed him, except I knew every school had stupid targets to keep to. He didn't really care about me – this was about the school doing well.

"Marty ... I thought we agreed that you were going to make an effort?"

We agreed? Since when did he agree anything? Did he have my life? Did he have to go to bed every night crapping himself about what his mum might do next? Did he wake up each day hoping it might be different? Did he go to a place where everyone thought he was some kind of nutter? Some kind of freak like his mum...

He sighed. "Are you going to talk to me?"

I shrugged again. "There's not much to say. I tried. I had to leave. I was wound up."

"Why were you wound up? Why didn't you come and find me?"

I sighed. "I'm not some grass and I'm not going to sit here whinging about other kids. I got stressed out. I dealt with it badly and I needed to get away, before—"

"Before what?"

I didn't answer. I was staring at the floor now, feeling heavy and tired. I was sick of fighting. Sick of all of this. I just wanted to be...

What did I want to be? Normal, I guess. Just normal.

Mr Terry looked at me and rubbed his eyes. "Marty, we both know the rumours that are flying around about you. Some of them are beyond ridiculous. I heard some year eight saying you'd murdered someone!" He snorted. "Word gets around but it also gets twisted, and it's up to you to show people who you really are. Instead you keep yourself away, and they get more suspicious of you. Does that make sense?"

"Yes. Of course it does."

"You had good friends before. Your reports from Greenfields said you were a popular kid until..."

"Kwaime."

"Until Kwaime," Mr Terry said in agreement.

"He used to be my best mate," I said, my voice sounding weak and pathetic, but I was beyond caring.

"But you weren't moved here just because of that incident, Marty. Your behaviour had been slipping for some time. You know that, don't you?"

I nodded.

"I would say it's been going on since your dad died. That happened when you were thirteen, right?"

I felt my body slump again. I wanted to lean against the wall and sink right into it – disappear. I didn't want to talk about this.

"Marty, I know I've said this before but I really think you should consider counselling. You need to talk to someone – you've been through so much. It's no wonder you're angry. Anyone would be."

"I don't *want* to talk to someone," I said, my words cold and brittle. "I don't want people thinking they can get into my head and poke around. I'm fine. I deal with things my way."

"But what if your way isn't working?" His voice was gentle now. "Please just think about it, Marty. And please keep trying at school. Come to me if you're stressed. I want to help."

I looked up. He was staring right at me; his eyes looked honest.

"You really want to help?" I asked, my voice husky, not even my own.

"Of course. Of course I do."

"Then help my mum, because I don't know how to."

That was the moment I finally sat down – practically falling into the chair. I rested my head on the table and felt my guilt wash over me like a sick wave. I was meant to protect Mum. That was my job. But I was tired. So tired. And scared, too.

Mr Terry stayed silent, and it wasn't until he handed me a box of tissues that I realized I was crying.

"Of course I'll help," he said. "Just talk to me."

As I walked up to the flat, I felt more defeated than ever. They say that when you tell people stuff you're meant to feel freer – lighter? Well, that's total crap. I was a lead weight. Sick chewed at my throat and worked itself down into the lining of stomach, clenching and clawing. I had betrayed her. I had grassed on my own mum in a moment of weakness. And what now? Mr

Terry would call the social and they would come sniffing tomorrow.

I'd ruined everything just to protect myself.

You're a screw-up. A liability.

You deserve everything that happens now.

Everything.

I heard her voice as I came to the door, loud and excitable. Was J back or was she talking to herself again?

"Angels come to save us! It's a sign. Everything is a sign – and you ... I knew it! I just knew something was going to happen. I was waiting. Waiting...! Look at you! Shining bright. You have to help me – tell me..."

It was only when I walked into the hall that I heard the second voice. Softer, trembling slightly. But familiar.

"I really think I need to go now."

My heart slammed into my guts.

No.

Not her.

What the hell was she doing here?

I ran into the kitchen. Mum was standing there,

almost pinning Daisy against the wall. Daisy looked so small in comparison, her red cheeks glowing against her white PE T-shirt. She must've come straight from school. But why? She had no right. How did she even know how to get here? She was trying to edge past Mum, trying to move under her arm. Her large, frightened eyes caught mine as I crashed into the room.

"Marty!" she said, and I could hear the panic in her voice. "I was waiting for—"

"What are you doing here?" My voice was loud – way louder than I wanted it to be. I watched Daisy blink in surprise, and shrink back a little. I was loud enough to make Mum turn around. Her face was glowing, and her face was fixed in a smile. Her eyes were moving erratically between us.

"She came, Marty. She came!" she said, pointing randomly. "I told you—I *told you* they'd send me a message. This is my sign. An angel from nowhere!"

Oh my God.

She's lost it. She's completely lost it.

I looked at Daisy, standing there in my pit of a kitchen, surrounded by mess and chaos. Cowering in front of this ranting, wild woman who was my mum. Shame raged through me.

Now she knows – she knows what a total mess my life is.

I shouldn't have to deal with this.

She shouldn't have come.

"Get out," I shouted at Daisy. I couldn't even look at her. I didn't want her to see me, here, in this place. "You shouldn't have come."

Kwaime – he came here. He saw everything, and look what happened.

"Marty—" Her voice was shaky but firm. She tried to come near me but I turned away.

"You shouldn't have come," I said again.

"She's an angel!" Mum said, her voice high and breaking.

"She's no one, Mum," I said. I didn't watch her leave, but I felt the slam of the door as it vibrated through the flat. It was only after Mum had flopped exhausted into the chair that I saw it lying there on the table.

Watership Down.

DAISY

That was not how was it meant to be. It wasn't.

Everything was a mess now. *Everything*. And I didn't even understand why.

I walked home, ignoring everything around me – just kept my head bent against the wind and tried not to look at anyone. I didn't want them to see I was crying. How had that even happened? I'd tried to do a nice thing but it was me who was made to feel bad. I hadn't done anything wrong.

Why was Marty so angry?

Why did he look like he hated me so much?

Had I got it so wrong about him?

I had waited for him after school. Waited

for ages and he hadn't shown up. Then I heard them talking – a gang of gobby kids mouthing off about some fight – and my ears pricked up when someone said Marty's name. They said he'd legged it out of school. I could've just gone home, but something told me not to. He might've needed to talk – he might've just needed a friendly face (ha!) – so I walked to his flat instead. I remembered the number from before. Thirty-three. My lucky number. I thought it was a sign. How wrong could I be!

Maybe I should've text him first – that might have been a smarter move. But I figured if he was wound up or upset he might've told me not to bother. I thought he wouldn't have minded. I guess I didn't really think it through.

I just wanted to be nice.

Stupid Daisy.

Stupid, stupid. . .

It was OK at first, when his mum came to the door. She was still in her pyjamas but Marty had said she'd been ill so I didn't think much of it. She was nice – she asked me my name and invited me in. Told me Marty wouldn't be long. Everything seemed fine.

Then she saw the book.

I was meant to give it to Marty first but she saw it and just grabbed it. That was when she went all strange. She said I must've been a messenger, that this had to be a sign. Only a messenger would know about "the book". She kept talking about my white top, saying I was pure, saying I was an angel. She said I was going to help her destroy the devil.

I tried to leave then. I tried to get away but she stopped me. And do you know what? I was scared, with her standing there, arms either side of me. I couldn't leave and she kept going on and on, telling me I was important.

And then Marty came back and I was so relieved. I thought he would sort it all out.

But instead he told me to go.

He looked like he hated me.

Well, maybe he was right – maybe I was no one.

No one to him, anyway.

By the time I got to my house I'd calmed down a bit. I'd stopped crying, at least. I had to be normal now – happy Daisy. If Mum and Dad found out about what had happened, they would freak and they really didn't need anything else to freak about.

It was quiet inside, but a familiar smell filled the house. Christmas. I pushed open the living-room door. There sat the Christmas tree, a real one proud in its pot. It smelt delicious. Of earth and green. Someone had already started to decorate it, as baubles lightly dripped on the lower branches. But it was half-finished. It looked odd and out of place.

Where was everybody?

Then I heard sounds in the kitchen. Quickly, I walked through. Something cold clenched my stomach. Something was wrong.

Nan was there, standing by the window and looking out at the garden. She turned as I moved into the room.

"Daisy," she said softly. "I didn't hear you."

Then she burst into tears.

Bad, dark, scary thoughts were flooding me. I was frozen. I knew as soon as I saw her there that this wasn't good. Nan only came when it was an emergency. Her being here was a bad sign.

"What is it? Tell me!" My voice was too loud. The words were shrill, forceful. I just wanted her to stop bloody crying and tell me what was happening.

Where was Harry?

"He – he had to be rushed in. Your mum called for an ambulance. Oh, Daisy, he wasn't breathing. He stopped breathing. . ."

No. Not again.

I swore loudly, and it was almost like *I* stopped breathing too; the air was stuck in my throat, gathering there like a thick knot. I had to force myself to suck it in, and I took a step back so I could cling to the kitchen side as the sickness clawed up from my stomach.

"How? Mum was so careful. We all were."

"We don't know," she said. "His cold had probably got worse. You know how weak his lungs are. . ."

How weak his *everything* is. His lungs. His muscles. His heart.

Twice this had happened before. Both times I'd been there to comfort him. *I had been with him.* But I hadn't been there this time. I'd been getting shouted at round that loser's place. Getting chased around the kitchen by his mental mum while my brother was fighting for his life.

"Why didn't they call me?" I sobbed. "I would've run home. I would've been there."

"It happened so quickly. Your mum only had time to call me. I raced down here but when I arrived they'd already gone."

I didn't want to hear any more. I wanted to get out of there. But where could I go?

I just wanted to be with Harry.

Nan sighed. "What can we do, anyway? We have to let the experts work on him now. We can't get in the way."

"But what if he—"

The words were stuck. I gasped again. This couldn't be happening.

"He won't," said Nan, and her voice was firm. She reached out and gripped my hand. "He's so tough. He'll fight. Just you wait and see."

"I want to see him."

I'd only been with him this morning, but it felt like a million years ago now. What had we done together? What had we said? Had I told him I loved him?

Oh God, I didn't think I had.

"Nan. . ." I moaned, and the tears were flooding out of me, I couldn't have stopped them, even if I'd wanted to. "I'm so scared."

She wrapped me up in her arms, held me close and slowly rocked me. I don't know how long we were like that. I didn't know I had that many tears to cry.

Three hours had passed and Mum still hadn't text. I had been pacing the living room, trying to fight the buzzing feeling that was working through my body. Every time my phone vibrated I leapt on it, but it was just Martha or Marty. I ignored them both without reading them.

I want my mum. I want her to tell me it's OK.

Nan made me a dinner that I couldn't eat. My stomach felt like it was inside-out, my throat glued tight. How could I force food down?

"I want to go to the hospital," I said finally.

"I'm not sure that's a good idea. It could be upsetting and they don't like too many family—"

"*I want to go to the hospital.*" My words were like splinters in my mouth. "He's my brother. I *need* to be with him."

Nan paused for a moment, assessing me. I could see the tiny frown mark appearing between her eyes. The same one Mum had. They were so alike. Two strong women. Two fighters.

"OK," she said. "Get your coat. I have to admit, sitting around here is driving me mad, too."

I picked up my phone as I was leaving, and automatically checked the screen. Another message from Marty – his second now. What was he doing – having another go at me?

I turned my phone off. I didn't need his grief right now. I had bigger worries.

But as I left the house, his words came back to me.

No one can guarantee their tomorrow.

Was the day I'd been dreading for so long finally here?

MARTY

She wasn't answering. I had text her three times and called her once and she hadn't answered.

You've screwed it up, you idiot.

You always do this. Why don't you bloody think before you start raging?

Because you never think. Never.

I hated this. I didn't mean to shout at her, but she shouldn't have shown up like that. The flat, Mum – that was my business. And now she knew how bad things actually were. There was no way I could go on pretending now.

And what does she think of me now, eh? There's no way in hell she'll come near me.

Mum seemed to be calmer, sort of. It was unnerving. J had called to say he'd be back later and she'd got this kind of glazed expression on her face, like she was stoned or half asleep, or something. She didn't look happy or sad, just weirdly blank.

I tried making her some food again, but there was hardly anything in the cupboards and I couldn't even think straight. Would out-of-date pasta shapes in tomato sauce be OK with crackers? Well, it was food. It would have to do.

Not that Mum cared. She took one spoonful and didn't even register what it was.

"Nice. That's so nice."

I stared down at the orange blobs in the bowl. They were meant to be space invaders, but they looked more like distorted faces. Mum probably bought these years ago, when I was younger. In the days when chicken nuggets and chips were my favourite meal. Mum had never been much of a cook, but she had tried.

Dad had been the chef, of course. Huge Sunday dinners. Bangers and mash. He'd loved his grub. I imagined him now, standing over me. Watching me trying to nibble a tomato-soaked cracker. What would he make of the pathetic mess we'd become?

"Mum, maybe you should – I dunno ... have a nice bath or something?" I shuffled in my chair. "J said he'd be back in a few hours. You wanna look nice, don't you?"

Not that he'd care. He'd be back down the pub within minutes. Sometimes I wondered why he bothered showing up here at all. But I guess this was a base for him. Somewhere he could leave his stuff. I didn't for one second believe he loved Mum.

Mum was playing with a strand of her hair and staring at me, that same fixed expression on her face. It was freaking me out a bit.

"Mum? Shall I run you a bath?"

"OK," she said finally, still smiling. "It's exciting, isn't it?"

"What is?"

"J, coming home."

I turned away. I didn't want her to see the doubt in my eyes. She'd been calling him a devil all week. But J had to come back. His things were still here. Besides, I needed to talk to him. I needed to tell him what I'd done. Guilt clawed at me at the thought.

Social services would be here tomorrow. They'd see Mum like this.

Oh God. What the hell had I done?

Luckily she was in the bath when J breezed in. He looked like he'd been on holiday all week, not on a building site. I obviously didn't look the same.

"Marty, mate. You look God-awful," he said as a greeting. "Where is she?"

I gestured towards the bathroom. It was quiet in there.

"Aw, good. I'm glad she's OK."

Seriously? Was he for real?

"She's *not* OK," I hissed. "She hasn't been sleeping, she hasn't been eating, and she's been saying really weird stuff—"

"Like what?" He raised an eyebrow, a tiny smile curling on his face. Did he actually think this was funny?

"Like, you're the devil and you're trying to kill us. That she's getting messages from the internet and the TV."

J snorted. "Ha! Maybe I am!"

"This isn't funny!" I seriously wanted to slap him. His smug grin was doing my head in – why did he think this was some kind of joke? What was he – two?

"Aw, mate!" He raised his arms up in defence. "Don't get all lippy on me. I'm tired, I just want to chill. I'm sure Jo's fine. You know how she gets. She's just highly strung."

"This is different. Worse than normal."

"Nah – she'll probably crawl into bed again for a few days and wake up fine. Tiredness gets to us all." He yawned as if to make a point and then yelled through the closed door. "Hey, Jo! I'm back!"

I heard splashing, and her muttering something.

"It's not just that, J, it's different this time. Mr Terry said she needs to see someone. A doctor."

He whirled over to face me, his cheeks pink. "What did you say?"

I back away a little. I could hear movements in the other room, Mum stomping about. I didn't want her to hear. "I just told him that I was struggling.

You don't know what it's been like – you weren't here!"

"I was *working*. Out earning," he sighed. "I've seriously had enough of this."

"I know, but—"

J slammed his hand against the wall. "Now, thanks to you we'll have the social back on our cases. They *can't* find out about my job. It's cash in hand. They could stop my benefit." His eyes were glaring at me. "You could ruin everything."

But this isn't about you... Can't you see?

THIS ISN'T ABOUT YOU!

The bathroom door swung open and Mum stepped out. She was completely naked and dripping from the bath, with clusters of bubbles still slipping off her pink skin.

"GO!" she shouted. And then I saw the flash of a blade in her hand. A knife glinting in the light.

A knife? How did she even...?

A knife. A blade.

What was going on?

J seemed rooted at the spot. I swear he was smiling again, rocking back on his heels. His hands went up in a "now, now'" way – as if he could back her off. But Mum (was this really Mum. *My mum?*) just made this strange wailing noise in her throat. It was horrible – animal-like.

And then she lunged at him.

The blade went high. Shining under the kitchen light, speeding down.

J screamed.

And I ran.

Bloody crazy coward, look at you running like a mug.

What do you think you're doing?

Where are you going?

Stop running.

Sort this.

Sort this now.

But I carried on moving. My legs seemed to take over. I watched my fingers punch out three numbers on my phone. I had to. I couldn't leave J up there alone with her. She could...

She *could*...

Air was pumping into my lungs and it was difficult to breathe, but I kept moving. Kept running. Down the stairs – so many stairs – and out of the tower block. The cold air hit me, a blast in the face, and at the same time a voice on the other end of the phone calmly asked me what service I needed.

What did I need?

Ambulance? Police? Both?

"It's my mum. She's gone crazy. She's stabbed him." I was choking out words. Coughing. Breathing too fast. "Please – I dunno – just help us."

I started coughing more; it felt like my lungs were on fire. I ran down the street, giving my address between bursts of air.

"What's your name?" she asked.

"Marty," I gasped. "Marty Field."

"How old are you? Where are you right now?"

I looked around me. I was in the centre of the estate by the green. Houses stood around me, some lit up with Christmas lights, others in darkness. The tower block stood in front of me – tall and imposing like a decaying chimney. I hated it. I hated everything about it. Inside – inside one of those boxes – it was chaos. *That* was my life.

I gave out my address. The words that tumbled out felt robotic and cold. How could this even be happening? Nothing felt real.

"We are sending someone out now, Marty. I just need to know: are you OK? Are you hurt? Are you in a safe place right now?"

The voice on the phone was soothing, but for a moment I wanted to scream down my mobile at her.

"Are you safe, Marty?" she asked again.

I stared around at the grey, familiar surroundings and fought back the urge to cry like some stupid kid. Safe? I didn't even know what safe was any more.

I hung up the call and pushed my mobile back into my pocket.

I didn't know where to go. I couldn't go home, everything was a mess and I couldn't face it. I couldn't face going back and finding out what she'd done. What if she...

Could she have...?

I pushed back the thoughts, hating the memory of that blade flashing in her hand. How could she do that? Go to hurt someone. Really hurt someone?

And J? I never thought she could do something like that.

Not my mum.

And now. Now there'd be police there, at our house, digging around, asking questions. What would they say when they saw me? What would they do with me?

What would they do with *Mum*?

I walked for a bit. I didn't have my coat and the wind bit at my skin. I was starting to feel sick and giddy. But it was quiet out, which was strange. Usually there'd be kids knocking about until late – hanging around the park or kicking a ball about the scrap of green we called a field. I needed this peace. How long had it been since I'd had quiet in my life? *Real* quiet? There was always too much noise, too much chaos. My head needed space. It needed to clear itself out.

I kept walking. Out of the estate. Along the main road and into town. Past the posh old houses. Houses where I wanted to live one day – when I could finally make money. I'd be a better person, have a decent place and a decent wage. I'd never have to eat dry crackers and pasta shapes again.

This would not be my life.

I'd walked here with Daisy just the other day. That seemed like months ago now. I remember how good I'd felt. My head started to ache. I wished she were here right now. What I wouldn't give to see her smile. It would help. I know it would.

But you screwed it up. You pushed her away.

I heard sirens.

What if...

What if she had...?

I forced back the thoughts. All I knew was that I couldn't go back. I couldn't. I couldn't see her again. Not like that.

Everything had changed.

I reached the end of the road where the bus stop was. My arms were white with cold, and my hands tingling and numb. But in my pocket was my last pound. It was enough. I sat myself in the bus shelter, huddled up in the seat trying to get some warmth back into my body. There was an old man sitting on the far end, holding his stick in front of him like it was keeping him upright. He was tiny, all skin and bone. His thin, white face turned to me and he smiled.

"Bloody bus is always late."

I nodded.

"You're not dressed for this weather. It's winter you know, son. You'll catch your death."

I pulled my arms tighter around me, but I didn't feel anything.

What had she done?

"I've seen that haunted look before. Is everything OK, son?" His voice was kind.

"No..." I whispered. "No, it's not."

"Oh." He paused, moving his stick around a bit on the ground. "Is it something you can fix?"

My mum? Can I fix her? Can I?

I shook my head. The cold was hitting me now. I was shivering – proper shivering.

"Well, if it's something you can't fix, you can't torture yourself," the man said gently. "You can only take care of the things you have control of. You've got to look after number one sometimes."

His stick was grinding on the ground as he

shifted about. "And look, our bus is here. Just in time. Do you know where you're going?"

I looked up as the bus swept in. Its number blazed on the front.

I hadn't known before, but I did now.

For once, I knew exactly where I was going.

DAISY

The room was small and smelt funny – like bleach and plastic and misery. The chairs were small, too, and rock hard. The walls were sterile white and glaring. I felt like I was going crazy, cooped up in this claustrophobic space. Waiting. Not knowing. Praying. I wasn't even religious, but I needed someone – something – to grab hold of. I needed *hope*. To be told it was going to be all right – that Harry would make it through. I wanted someone to take my hands in theirs and promise me – *promise me* – that this would all be over soon.

Instead, all I could see was sad, lost faces. Nan was sat next to me, her hands locked together on her lap, staring at the closed door. There was another family sat at the far side of the room. Another mum and dad? She had been crying, her eyes red and her face blotchy. He kept reaching over to stroke her hand, his face frozen as he stared into space.

This was the room of broken hearts. Where they put people to wait, and hope, and worry, and think the worst. Time seemed to pass slowly here. The air was heavy and thick. The rest of the world was gone. It was just us, in one small room, trapped with our own thoughts.

The last time we were here, I think I had been more hopeful. Less scared. I think I might have even been sitting in the same chair. The last time, I'd had Mum there with me – strong Mum, holding my hand, saying the right things, telling me it'll be OK.

But this time Mum wasn't here. She and Dad were with Harry. They were allowed to sit with him. Watch over him.

I wasn't.

I just wanted to be with my little brother.

I *needed* to be with him.

*

I don't know how long it was, maybe a few hours after we arrived, but finally Dad walked into the room. He looked awful – *really* awful. Like a ghost. I immediately threw myself at him, not caring what anyone else thought.

"Dad! What's going on? I couldn't stay at home. I couldn't just..."

Dad held me tight, softly murmuring something that I couldn't quite hear. I pulled back. "What?"

He peered down at me, his eyes so sad and lost-looking. "You need to go home," he said gently. "It's no use being here. Mum is with Harry now; she won't leave his side."

"What do you mean?"

Nan came up behind me. "What's going on, Chris? What are they saying?"

Dad kept one arm wrapped around me while he gripped the back of the chair. I could see the tips of fingers turning white.

"There's no change, he's still critical. We just have to wait and see."

His voice cracked on the last word.

Wait and see? What did that even mean? Why couldn't they just *do* something?

"I don't understand. He was fine this morning. Everything was fine. How could it get so bad?" Words were flying out of my mouth and I couldn't stop them. I needed to know – I needed to understand.

Dad sighed and rubbed his forehead. Oh God, he looked so tired.

"The doctors think he has an enterovirus. It's something anyone can get, but for Harry it's much more serious. It means he has a build-up of fluid around his heart and his lungs are struggling to cope. His muscles are tired. His body is shutting down."

Shutting down.

I wanted to puke. This couldn't be real.

This couldn't be happening.

I heard Nan talking – asking more questions – but it was all becoming a blur in my mind. A tangle of noise. I couldn't deal with this.

"I can't go home," I said, and my voice sounded thick. "I can't."

My dad's arm gripped me again. "Please. I need you there, safe. This is no place to be. Please, Daisy. I promise we'll call if anything changes."

"But I need to see him."

"I know," he whispered.

He didn't say what we were both thinking.

That I might never see Harry again.

Back home, back in my room, I lay down and listened to the silence. The gaps left by those who weren't there. I could almost hear them, if I concentrated hard enough: Dad, joking and singing some rubbish old song; Mum, stressing and having a go about something; Harry laughing, or having a meltdown because his favourite show wasn't on TV. Usually those noises did my head in. But not today. Today I longed to have them back. I wanted to be encased by them. This emptiness was killing me.

"Killing me."

Bad turn of phrase, Daisy.

I messaged Martha for a bit and she was sweet enough. I guessed it helped a little. She said the right things – that she was sorry, and that she was there if I needed her – but, I don't know, part of me felt like they were just words. Just something to say. I didn't really believe her. I read Marty's messages too. The first was just an apology, the second was much of the same – saying that he was "out of order" and "all over the place" and asking to talk.

The third was different.

> Daisy. I won't keep hassling you, but I want to explain.

> Some stuff has happened... I don't want to do this over text.

> If you're interested get back to me, yeah?

I started to type out a reply, but I didn't know how to start. What could I say?

"Hey, Marty, we *could* chat but I'm kind of

distracted right now."

Or, "Hey, Marty. Yeah you're a bit of knob but I kind of have other things on my mind..."

I threw my phone to the end of my bed and crept out of the room, quietly pushing open the door next to mine.

Harry's bed was so comforting – so familiar. I gently eased myself on it, pulling the duvet towards me so I could breathe in the smell of him. If I closed my eyes I could imagine he was there. I always kissed him goodnight – it was my ritual, it kept him safe. But tonight I couldn't.

Come back soon, bubs.

Come home to us.

Let everything be OK again.

I gripped his stupid dog, Dudley, in my hands. So tatty and grey, but it was Harry's. It smelt only of him. It should have been with him, nestled in his arms. I kissed the worn-out nose, imagining it was Harry's nose instead.

"Sleep tight, little man."

I can't remember falling asleep. But when I did I dreamt of him.

MARTY

When I woke up, I didn't know where I was at first. My bed was facing the wrong way. The room was smaller and cleaner, and it was so quiet. But it didn't take long for the events of the night before to come spilling back into my head. I closed my eyes, praying for more sleep, but if course it didn't come. I had to get up. Get on. Face up to it all.

Last night, Jackie had listened to everything I told her with very little surprise. I guess she always thought this day might come. At first she didn't even ask questions – she just pulled me into a tight hug and offered me a drink, food, a bath – whatever it was I needed. I really liked it at her house. I hadn't come back there for years, not since Dad was alive. We used to visit a lot, though – Dad liked watching the football with Jackie. But after Dad died, Mum never came and she didn't want me to, either. She always thought Jackie judged her, which made no sense to me. I guess a lot of Mum's thinking made no sense.

That was all becoming a bit clearer to me now.

I'd knocked on her door last night because I didn't know where else to go. I was so stressed – so worried – that it all burst out of me in a tidal wave of words.

"She went at him!" I yelled. "She went at him with a blade. I didn't know what to do."

I was crying, I think, but Jackie was so calm. She sat me down, made me take breaths. I felt like a kid again. A stupid baby, sitting there. I should've sorted my mum out, pulled her off J or something – not run away.

"I called the police," I said finally. "They'll arrest Mum. That's it! She'll never forgive me."

Jackie breathed hard. "Shit. . . Oh, Marty, you poor thing."

"I didn't know what to do…"

"You did the right thing, Marty," she told me. And it was so good to hear someone say that. "She had a knife. If you'd stayed in there, you could have got hurt too."

She saw me take a big gasp of air, and held up her hands to calm me.

"It would've been by accident, obviously. Your mum's not thinking clearly right now."

She hesitated for a bit, then asked gently, "Marty, how long has she been like this? I mean, this bad?"

"I dunno, on and off since Dad died." I gulped. "I mean. At first she was just crying a lot. She'd spend a few days in bed, and not talk much, but that wasn't so bad. Then J started coming over. He was one of Dad's old mates. She got really happy then, and for a bit she was OK again and talking loads about plans and all the things we could do together. But when J started working, she went weird. First it was long times in bed and then it was *days* on the internet, looking for signs that people were out to get her. Then she starting saying J was the devil, or something."

Jackie didn't say anything for a bit. She kept rubbing my leg and making those hushed noises adults do to kids who've hurt themselves. I'd normally find it patronizing but, weirdly, I didn't care. I was beyond caring.

She got up. "I need to make some calls," she said.

I don't how long she was out of the room, but it felt like ages. I remember sinking back into her comfy sofa, wanting to disappear completely. Across the room was a framed picture of Dad smiling right at me. He was younger in it, but he still looked how I remembered: dark hair, big goofy grin.

"I'm sorry, Dad," I whispered. "I screwed up. But I couldn't do it any more."

Jackie walked back into the room. "I managed to speak to someone," she said. "J is stable. Your mum did stab him – and the knife caught J on the shoulder. But the ambulance got to him quickly. He will be fine."

I breathed, letting Jackie's words sink in. "And Mum?"

Jackie sighed. "I'm not sure. The police said she's in their custody. They were pleased to hear you're with me. They said someone would come talk to us in the morning."

I let this happen. If I'd looked after her properly. . .

"Marty," Jackie said softly, as if she was reading my mind. "You did the right thing. She's ill. She needs help." She drew out a shaky breath. "I just hadn't realized how bad things had got. I'm so sorry."

I looked up at her. "Why are you sorry?"

"For not stepping in sooner. You told me it was all OK and I chose to believe you. . ." I could see the tears in her eyes. "But I should have known better. I know Jo struggled after your dad died—"

"I wanted to help her. She had wobbles before, but Dad got her through it – I thought I could too."

"But this is *different*, Marty. This isn't a wobble." Jackie said. "I really think your mum needs specialist help now. It can't be just you supporting her."

Jackie phoned the school. Made it official.

"You're not going in today," she said, making me some breakfast. "Just look at the state of you."

I nodded, relieved. I knew I'd have to face it

soon. But that was a battle for another day.

"You're sure J will be OK?" I asked.

"He was lucky. Your mum caught him a few times on his arm and shoulders. Some nasty lacerations. He'll need stitches." Jackie sighed. "But hopefully there will be no long-term damage."

"I don't know how this happened."

Jackie laid out my toast carefully, taking her time.

"I don't know, sweetheart. I remember your dad telling me that she suffered from depression but she didn't want to go to a doctor... Maybe that intensified with the pressure of your dad's death? I'm only guessing. But what I do know is that she needs proper medical help."

"And now social services will be here." My stomach suddenly went hard. "They won't let me stay with her now, will they?"

"She might not be allowed home for a bit, Marty."

"I'll live on my own, then. I can cope."

"It's not as easy as that." Jackie nibbled on her toast. "You need to listen to what they say."

"They just want to interfere – ruin our lives."

Jackie sighed again. "Marty, you have to stop this. Stop pushing people away. If you'd told someone how bad things were getting your mum might've got help sooner." Her voice was firm now. "Social services aren't the big bad beast here. They just want to keep you and your mum safe. And if your dad was here he would be saying the same thing. He'd be begging you to stop being so stubborn and accept help. You're *sixteen*, Marty. You're too young to screw up your life."

I bent my head, chewing the toast that suddenly felt like paper.

"Your dad was so proud of you," Jackie went on. "So proud. He'd hate to see you like this – angry, fighting at school, missing lessons. He would want to see you striving, Marty. Succeeding. Trying to do the best for yourself."

"I am," I muttered. "But Mum—"

"Your mum will get the professional help she needs. This is your chance to put yourself first. You need to show the world that Marty Field is not a waste of space. You need to fight back."

But I *was* a waste of space. Couldn't she see that? Couldn't everyone see that?

The toast scratched the sides of my throat as I swallowed it.

Jenny and her trusty sidekick Debbie arrived at ten a.m. sharp. I was sat in the spare room at the time, staring at my phone. I guess I was hoping that Daisy would've text back by now.

Wake up, sad case. She's not interested in your lame excuses.

Give up.

I heard their high-pitch voices outside my room, all fake-happy "lovely to meet you" stuff. I wondered if they were always like that. Even when they were coming in to wreck your life, take you away from your family – did they still wear their forced smiles and greet you with a sickly sweet hello?

Just go away. Piss off. I don't need this.

But I couldn't hide away. What was the point? I knew the longer I waited in my room, the worse it would be. The feeling gnawed away at my stomach. I bet if they took an X-ray of my insides there would be a hole there – a great big gaping hole – an empty space where my guts used to be.

I took a deep breath and stepped outside.

"Where's my mum?"

Jenny was sat on the sofa facing me, with Debbie sitting on the chair making notes. I saw that Jackie had made them teas. She was standing up and looked nervous. Her arms were crossed in front of her. Jenny looked up and smiled at me – that bright smile again. I swear I wanted to slap it away. I had to bite my lip. Take another deep breath. I realized I was shaking.

"Hello, Marty. Thanks for coming out," she said. "I'm really glad you're here. You had us worried for a bit last night – we didn't know where you were." She paused. "But it was you who called the ambulance, wasn't it?"

I nodded. "Yeah. I didn't want to, though – I knew she wouldn't hurt him really."

Jenny's eyebrow went up slightly. Just a touch, before she composed herself. Her face was dead serious.

"Really, Marty? Did you *really* know that?"

I stared at the floor. I couldn't answer that, not truly, and she knew it.

Of course she would've hurt him, you idiot. She had a blade. She was proper raging. She was always going to stab him.

"Your mum isn't well," Jenny said.

Her voice had lost the sweetness now. It was just soft. Even so, each word hit my skin and floated into the deep hole where my guts had been, making me feel heavier and sicker than before.

"She was still angry when the police came. They couldn't calm her down and they had to bring in reinforcements. Marty, your mum has been taken to a hospital where she will be getting treatment and help. She has been sectioned. Do you understand what that means?"

I stared at her open mouthed. All I could see was straitjackets and padded cells. I wanted to scream. Cry. Shut this stupid cow up.

"She will be looked after, Marty. She will get the correct treatment and care, and she will have time to recover. She needs this. You both need this."

Sectioned. That's what happens to mad people, isn't it? Lunatics. Nutters.

But this was my mum.

"NO!" I shouted out. "You can't do this to her. I can look after her."

Jenny stood up then and walked over to me. Her hand lightly touched my arm. I wanted to push her arm away but oddly I didn't.

"Marty. You can't look after her. Your mum needs *specialist* help. You know that really, don't you?"

I could feel myself sinking, sinking. "But what about me? What happens to me?"

"Well" – Jenny's hand was still on me, gently holding me – "your aunt has offered to look after you and we can trial that for a bit. See how it goes. I mean we need to do all the checks, but I can't see why—"

"I'd love to have you here, Marty," Jackie said. "It's what your dad would've wanted."

Dad. My dad.

"I miss him so much," I said.

And then I was proper crying and I didn't care. I didn't care that they all saw and I didn't care when Jackie came and wrapped me in her arms.

I didn't care about any of that.

I just wanted my life back.

My life.

DAISY

I was numb. Staring at a silent phone waiting to hear something. *Anything*. Or maybe not. Maybe I *didn't* want to hear anything. Maybe that was the last thing I wanted.

I didn't know any more.

I had barely slept. My body ached for rest but my mind refused to close down. It had to be alert. It had to be ready.

Nan wanted me to go to school, but how could I? There was no way my mind could focus on anything other than this. So I stayed at home, wrapped up on a sofa, lost in my worries, watching rubbish daytime TV and pretending to read a little of my school books.

I felt ... Well, I don't know how I felt.

Lost.

Yes, that.

Stupidly lost.

My mobile sat in front of me, its blank screen taunting me. I kept swiping it, like that would make Mum call us. But it was completely lifeless. Even Martha didn't text me.

Marty didn't, either.

I opened up his last message to me, the one he sent yesterday. I reread the words and imagined him sitting there typing it out. I wondered how he felt. Was he really sorry for shouting at me, or was he still a bit cross at me?

I want to explain.

I thought of his flat – of the chaos there, the mess. I remembered his mum, her wild behaviour, the way she had pushed me up against the counter. Said all those weird things, made me feel scared.

It must be hard for Marty, living like that. I know he didn't talk to many people about it.

Without thinking I typed out my reply.

OK, explain.

And then I waited.

But the screen turned dark and my mobile stayed silent.

No one was coming back to me.

I was alone.

After lunch I went for a walk, keeping my phone clamped in my hand. I had to get out of the house. I felt like I was going crazy in there – like I was running out of air or something. Nan had settled herself in the living room, watching some film. I don't think she was taking it in though, not really – her eyes were far away.

"Where will you go?" she asked.

"Just around the park. I need to clear my head."

"What if they call?"

And what if they don't? I can't just sit here, waiting like a useless lump.

"I have my phone. Ring me, I'll come back straight away," I said. "Please don't go anywhere without me."

"Of course I won't."

I slammed out of the house and on to the street.

It was quiet, which I liked. The road was clear of cars and there was hardly anyone about. There was a cold, icy breeze that stung my face. I had to keep my head down to stop my eyes watering.

As I walked I kept glancing at my phone, willing it to buzz from a message. I knew Mum would only text me if there was good news. This silence wasn't a good sign – not at all.

As for Marty, I figured he was just in a mood. I should've guessed that – it had been hours now and he hadn't bothered to reply. Well, screw him. I had more important things to worry about.

I kicked a beer can out of the path and watched it roll across the gutter. The gutter itself was full of leaves and other gunk, and I paused for a bit, caught in a stare.

How long ago was it when me and Harry had stood in the same place, poking our sticks through the metal casing? Was it only a year ago? I'd told Harry that a dragon lived down there and that the rainwater tamed his fire and kept us safe.

"What's his name?" Harry had whispered.

"No one knows. We think he's huge. The size

of a bus, maybe. Some people say he's red and others think he's green. But only a few have actually seen him."

"I bet he's red," Harry had said. "That's my favourite colour. And he would glow red like the fire in his belly."

"That sounds about right."

"And his name is Clive. Like the nurse at the hospital. Clive has red hair, too."

I'd nodded. "Clive is a great dragon name."

But Harry had looked sad all of a sudden. I remember squeezing his hand, asking him if he was all right.

"Clive is trapped in the drains. He can't move properly. He shouldn't be down there. He should be flying."

"I guess he's used to it," I said. "He probably doesn't mind."

"He wants to fly," he said, his voice soft. "I bet he dreams about flying every day."

I walked for over an hour, until my muscles ached and my face was numb with cold. I walked until

I couldn't bear to be outside any longer. Somehow it was like the air itself had become suffocating. I needed to be inside again, safe and tucked away.

And my phone remained silent. Part of me wanted to fling the useless thing against the nearest wall.

Just ring, stupid thing! Ring and tell me something. The nothing is too much.

I walked back towards the house, and stood at the door while my cold fingers fumbled with my key. My eyes drifted towards the front-room window. I could see our unfinished tree sitting there, waiting to be decorated properly. It looked so sad and forgotten. My stomach twisted inside me.

Harry loves that stupid tree, all lit up and looking pretty.

I wanted to walk inside and rip the stupid thing down, branch by branch.

I heard the voices as soon as I stepped in the hall. It made me pause for a second – who the hell was that? The rolling feeling in my stomach hadn't gone – in fact it felt worse. The voice was male, deep. But not Dad.

I hesitated.

Then I heard the soft laugh. One of those polite ones that people tend to do when they're nervous or not sure how to answer something. I recognized it instantly.

Marty.

Why the hell are you here? Go away.

You shouldn't have come.

I didn't ask you.

The irony burned at me. Did he do this on purpose? Rock up at my house because that's what I did to him? Normally I wouldn't have minded, but this was not a normal time! I couldn't deal with this right now.

I caught sight of my reflection in the hall mirror and barely recognized myself. I looked like I'd just been dug up. My hair was unbrushed and pulled into a bun. Spots lined my forehead above my glasses, planted on my pale un-made-up face. But what did it matter, really? I didn't care.

I walked into the room.

Marty was sat awkwardly on the sofa, holding a cup of tea. He turned as I came in. Nan was opposite him. She smiled at me.

"Daisy, you're back. I was beginning to worry."

"I said I would be fine. I just needed a walk." My eyes darted to Marty. "Why are you here?"

"Don't be rude, Daisy," Nan said coolly. "Your friend popped over to see you – you could at least say hello."

"Your nan told me about Harry," Marty said softly. "I'm so sorry."

I studied him for a bit. He looked different somehow – I don't know ... smaller? Shrunken. Like he'd lost a ton of weight, which was daft because I'd only seen him the other day. His hair was still a crazy mess, but there were more shadows under his eyes. He looked like he'd barely slept.

Nan seemed to sense the awkwardness. "I'll make you a drink too," she said to me, touching my arm. "And I'm going to try ringing the hospital again. See if there's any news."

I nodded and watched as she left the room but stayed where I was by the door. I didn't feel able to sit with him. This all seemed weird and wrong.

Marty put his drink down and stood up, burying his hands in his pockets.

"Maybe I should go – maybe I was wrong to come here ... I just wanted to—"

"What? What did you want to do?" My words were spiky. I knew they were but I couldn't help it.

"I – well, I know things got a bit out of line at mine..."

"Out of line!" I said, my voice wobbling now. "You threw me out, Marty. You made me feel like I'd done the worst thing in the world. I was just trying to be nice."

"You were being nice! That book – getting that book ... but I just ... I just couldn't deal with it. With you being there, and seeing it all. I'm sorry."

His body was slumping now.

"I can deal with it," I said softly.

"But *I* can't," he bit back. I'd never heard him say anything like that before – what exactly had happened since I last saw him?

"Your mum is nothing to be ashamed of, you know."

"Would you seriously be happy bringing people back to that?"

"I don't know," I answered honestly. "I guess

I'd hope someone might've helped us before it got that bad."

"She never used to be like this, though – I used to be able to manage her moods. But it's got more extreme lately. They think it's because of my Dad's death, money worries – a mixture of everything that all got too much for her."

"*They?*" I stared at him.

"Social services." He shrugged. "I am getting help now. Something happened the other night – it was really bad, Daisy. My mum lost it."

I felt a chill run down my spine. Marty's face was so pale. "Are you OK?"

He shrugged. "I guess . . . I dunno. I'm still trying to get my head round it. Daisy, she stabbed J."

I gasped. "Oh my God, Marty. Is he all right?"

"Yeah. Yeah, he's fine, but Mum . . . I don't think. . ."

His words trailed off. Words swam around in my head as I tried desperately to think of the right ones to say. In the end all I could find was, "I'm so sorry."

He came over towards me, his eyes catching

mine. So sad. So regretful. I could've lost myself in the dark brown swirls. He felt like someone I'd known for ever.

Jesus, Daisy, get a grip.

But actually, I didn't want to. For the first time in so long I could feel warmth creeping back inside my body.

"I'm so sorry, Daisy. I never meant to hurt you," he said.

"I know that now."

"And Harry will be OK, I just know it."

"You can't know that. You can't."

"Yes," he said, pulling me into his arms. "Yes I can."

And right then – in that moment – that was the only place I wanted to be.

MARTY

It felt good to hold her. I guess I'd wanted to for a long time. I let go of her slowly and finally looked at her properly. She looked different today – not bad different, but it was as if someone had rubbed some of the colour out of her. Her hair was pulled back and I could see the sharp curves of her cheekbones more clearly, and her eyes ... her eyes were so sad. It made my ache inside to see her like that.

"It's not the same, I know," I said. "But this whole situation with Mum has made me realize that I have to take each day at a time. I can't keep worrying about the stuff I have no control over."

She nodded, and a strand of hair loosened and fell in front of her face.

I shrugged. "I try to keep busy with other stuff now. Today I helped Jackie sort out new stock for the stall. It stops my mind thinking too much ... I dunno, sometimes thinking isn't such a good thing."

A tiny smile escaped from her. "You? Thinking too much? Surely not."

"I know. It's a scary thought but it does happen."

I looked over at their Christmas tree. It was only half decorated and that was really bugging me. Beside it stood a bucket full of decorations.

"Come on," I said, reaching for her. "Let's finish the tree. Make it really nice in here."

She shifted a little. "But it doesn't feel right, not without Harry here."

"Wouldn't it be nice for him to come home to a house all lit up like a grotto?" I said. "Wouldn't that be the best surprise after being in hospital?"

She bit her lip. "But he might not ... Marty, he might not..."

I grabbed her arm. I felt that spark inside me – the spark that reignited each time I got knocked down – again and again. The spark that refused to go away.

"He *will* be OK, Daisy. Don't even dare to think different."

I grabbed the decorations.

Daisy's nan came in with more drinks and even she smiled when she saw what we were doing.

"That'll look lovely," she said. "It's such an impressive tree."

It was too, one of those really huge real ones. It was certainly nothing like the pound-shop disaster that me and Mum had. That one didn't even stand up straight – we had to prop it against the TV last year. We had laughed about it, though, called it our "twiglet tree". We had still made it special.

We did have good Christmases. We did. She always made an effort. Got me a little present. Watched a film (Back to the Future, again!) and we would always have a nice day. Just us.

But what about this year? Where would she be? Would she be allowed home, or would it be just me and Jackie?

"Oi!" Daisy said, as I tried to reach over her. "You just elbowed my back."

"I wanted to get this red one over there." I pointed, then laughed. "Oh my God, you're hopeless at this. You put all the same colours together!"

"No I don't!" she said, sticking a silver bauble next an identical one.

"They should alternate. You don't want two of the same together."

"You have OCD."

"*You* have no eye for design."

She punched me lightly in stomach. "Idiot."

"Yeah, well that's true."

"Your mum will be so happy with you, Daisy," her nan said softly. "You've saved her a job."

Daisy turned around. "Have you got through to them yet?"

Her nan shook her head. "I tried the hospital. They said there was little change. Your mum's mobile is still off. It's just a waiting game."

Daisy was staring down at the tiny red bauble in her hand. "She must be so tired."

"Yes, yes, she must. And your dad, too."

I reached into the bucket of decorations and pulled out a wooden creation. It was covered in glitter and had cotton wool balls stuck to it. It looked like some weird mess, but Daisy immediately snatched it off me.

"Be careful with that one!"

"Sorry, Daisy. I just found it in there." I stepped back. "What is it anyway?"

She studied it a little. "I'm not sure, to be honest. Harry made it for me two years ago. It's kind of special."

She was just standing there staring at it, getting that lost look in her face again, so I slowly took it off her.

"Well, if it's special, it should go up here," I said, and I carefully reached up and placed it in the topmost branches. I have to admit, it was pretty freaky looking, but even so, Harry's star was going to shine brightly on top of their tree this year.

The tree looked great, as did the other Christmassy things that we'd put around the house. If it wasn't for the underlying feeling of sadness, you could almost believe it was festive in here.

Almost.

"Thank you," said Daisy, looking around. "It's great. It really is. Harry will love it."

I smiled. "I guess I should make a move. I have to catch a bus back to Jackie's; she's on the other side of town."

"Oh – I didn't realize."

We stood awkwardly for a bit in the room of twinkling lights.

"I'll walk to the bus stop with you," said Daisy. "I need to get out again."

The bus stop was only ten minutes away, and for most of it we walked in silence. It was late afternoon and getting dark already. All around us houses were lit up flashing their bright lights. Welcoming in winter.

"I don't want to go back," Daisy said suddenly. We'd reached the corner of the road where my bus stop was. The park was the far side.

"Come on," I said, taking her hand in mine.

"Won't you be late?"

"Only a little. It's fine."

We walked through the main entrance and over

the big sweep of grass. I liked it in this park. Paths criss-crossed the landscape and a large water fountain stood in the centre. It felt like the air here was cleaner and the sky was brighter. It was a good place to be.

I took us to a bench by the fountain, one that was tucked away from the main path. We huddled together.

"Why don't you want to go back?" I asked finally.

"I just can't. Everything reminds me of Harry and all I can do is think. Thinking is the worst. I know you said—"

"Yeah well, I said it, but it's not easy to turn the thinking off. I understand that."

She moved her body closer to me. I could feel her shiver. "One day, he will die. I know we *all* die eventually, but Harry's life expectancy is so low that we have to expect it to happen sooner. Every day is a waiting game. Can you even imagine what that's like?"

"No ... No, I can't."

"I hate it all. I hate seeing him in pain. He doesn't deserve that. He's too little to put up with so much. But he just gets on with it. You know, he has the sweetest smile? It breaks my heart."

"He sounds amazing."

"He is. And I love him so much..." Her voice was wobbling, breaking apart. "What if I never get to be with him again? How can I live without my little brother?"

Crap. What do I say? What's the right thing to say?

We were both staring at the fountain. At the rushing roar of the water over the concrete plinth. It was soothing somehow.

"It's not like that, though, is it?" I said finally.

"What?" She shifted, like I'd woken her.

"It's not like every day is a waiting game." I paused. "Surely every day you have is a good thing. Every day is another day you have with him. Remember what I told you before—"

"No one is guaranteed a tomorrow," she whispered.

I was surprised she remembered. "Yes – that. I never want to forget it." I reached for her hand and took it in my mine. It was so small. So cold. "In a way it's similar for me. With Mum I never know what she'll be like one day from the next.

I used to resent it all, but I know that I need to enjoy the good times when I can."

She squeezed my hand. "Yes."

"And when Dad died..."

Jeez, I was doing this. I was actually doing this.

"...when he died, I just lost the plot. It wasn't expected. He was hit by a car in the street. Killed instantly. How are you even meant to deal with that? I didn't get a chance to say goodbye, to enjoy being with him while he was here..."

My voice was shaky. I sounded like a mug but I didn't care. Her hand was still in mine, and she held on tighter now.

"We had a row the day he died. I told him I hated him. Mum even heard. We rowed because I hadn't picked up some dirty towels in the bathroom. I wanted Mum to do it – how lame is that? He left the house, thinking I hated him and I could never tell him..."

"I'm sorry," she said. And I knew she meant it.

"Don't dread each day. Just enjoy them – each one – with Harry. Right now, he's still here. I'd give anything to have one more day with Dad."

We sat and watched the water, her body now heavy against mine, our hands locked together. Both lost in our own thoughts, but weirdly supporting each other. It was OK.

I would be OK.

"I don't usually talk about this stuff," she said softly. "Things about Harry. I usually keep it locked away, but this is helping."

"You should talk about it. You are allowed to, you know."

"I know," she sighed. "I just don't like burdening other people with it all. But you seem to just get it. You understand."

"I have my uses!"

She gently squeezed my hand. I took that to mean that she agreed with me.

I liked that.

When her phone rang we both jumped. She pulled it out and stared at it for a bit. Her whole body was rigid.

"I can't – it's Mum – I can't," she said.

"You can," I said, nudging her.

She swiped the phone and answered tentatively.

I tried not to listen but she wasn't saying much anyway, her whole body was slumped forward as she muttering into the mobile.

"OK."

"OK?"

"Yeah..."

And then silence as she kept on listening. I was crapping myself for her. I picked up a stick and started ramming the ground with it.

Come on. Just tell her. Put her out of her bloody misery.

Then finally, "OK, Mum. Love you. Bye."

The phone went down in her lap and she drew a shaky breath.

"Well!" I spun towards her. "What is it? What did they say?"

"They said – they said – oh God..." Her breathing was all over the place. She took both my hands in hers. She was shaking and really crying now. "They said that he's improving. The drugs are kicking in and..."

"And?"

"I don't know ... I mean, it's still early days,

but he's fighting. That has to be a good sign, right? He's really fighting."

"Yes ... that's totally a good sign."

Tears were pouring from her now. I was even struggling to control my own emotions. She kept jiggling my hands, squeezing them in hers.

"I can't believe ... I was really starting to think... You know ... I was really starting to think that we might lose him ... That this was it."

She gasped, and put her hands over her face. "He can't go now. Not yet, Marty. I'm not ready."

I pulled her towards me, her still-shaking body, and held her close. I could feel her hot breath on my neck. She was like a fragile little bird.

I pulled back. "It'll be OK now," I said. "I told you it'll be OK."

She nodded. "I hope so."

"You said it yourself, he's a fighter."

"I know. I did."

As she leant over to kiss me I nearly fell back in shock, but luckily I recovered myself in time. Her lips were on mine and it was the best feeling ever, so soft at first and then harder, more urgent. Her tongue slipped into my mouth and I felt another spark light up inside me. I could taste her tears.

Oh, God. I really like this girl.

I really, really like this girl.

When we stopped, she took my hand again. "You're pretty cool, you know,"

"So are you."

She giggled and pulled me up towards her. "Come on, we better go. I'm going to decorate Harry's room for when he gets home. Light it all up. Make this the best Christmas ever!"

And maybe I could do some things too. Find something pretty Mum might like to have while she's in hospital. I know Jackie will help. Maybe Daisy will, too.

Perhaps this Christmas won't be so bad.

"Thank you for today," Daisy said as we walked back. "It's helped so much – all of this. More than you know."

"It wasn't a problem, honestly," I said.

"I'm really going to focus on living for today," she said, in a voice that sounded like a mixture of determination and sadness. "We both should."

I squeezed her hand. "I'm totally up for that."

We carried on walking, her hand locked tightly in mine. It felt good. Warm.

Right.

There were no more words, just a gentle silence that washed over us. And that was OK. I didn't need to talk now. I just needed this.

I thought of Dad. I thought of him walking alongside us. His eyes bright eyes, his laughing face turned towards me.

"Some things – some people – make the world that little bit brighter, more beautiful."

Yeah, Dad. You were right.

They do.

ACKNOWLEDGEMENTS

This is always the hardest part for me, as I have so many people to thank and I hate to think that I would miss anybody. But please remember that I'm grateful for everyone that has helped me, made me laugh and supported me on this wonderful and surprising journey.

I am truly grateful to all the people whose encouragement has helped shape *Tender* into the book it has become. Particular thanks go to the amazing people at Scholastic. I have been fortunate to work with two lovely, understanding and completely patient editors – Gen and Fiz. I am very lucky and you both deserve medals! Thanks also to Sam Smith, Olivia and Jamie, my wonderful cover designer. You all rock and I am so happy to be part of the team.

Thanks also to Stephanie Thwaites at Curtis Brown for continuing to be a professional and supportive agent.

My continuing thanks and love to my friends and family – in particular to Tom, who is my constant rock and sanity. He also makes great tea! And to Iain who has read so many drafts of my work he must be sick of it all, but never complains (at least not to me!) – I'm so thankful. And to my mum, for just being – Mum!

A shout-out to my author friends who have battled alongside me – you know who you are and I love you dearly. And thank you to the bloggers and librarians who continue to support and champion reading. You are awesome, honestly!

A big thank you to Ella and Ethan for making me laugh when I needed to and reminding me what it is important.

I was also so thrilled to be awarded an Arts Council grant in order to allow me time to write this novel, so would like to take this opportunity to say a huge THANK YOU for giving me the opportunity.

I would also like to acknowledge two special people. The first, Becky, opened up to me about mental health and some of her personal experiences. I appreciated her honesty and insight. Becs, you are amazing.

The other, Vicky, talked to me about her experiences of Muscular Dystrophy and the impact it has on her young son and her family. Vicky and her family are some of the most inspiring and dedicated people I've ever met. And if this book can even raise a teeny tiny bit more awareness about this truly heartbreaking condition, I will feel I've achieved something.

Tender is a work of fiction, but the issues raised are very real for many families and young people. If you do feel affected by the themes raised, please see the below list of charities and organisations to follow that can offer advice and support.

Keep smiling. Keep hoping. Keep reading

YOUNG CARERS
carers.org/about-us/about-young-carers

MUSCULAR DYSTROPHY UK
musculardystrophyuk.org

YOUNG MINDS
youngminds.org.uk

RETHINK
rethink.org

Eve Ainsworth has worked extensively in Child Protection and pastoral care roles, supporting teenagers with emotional and behavioural issues. She is also the author of *Seven Days, Crush and Damage*. Eve lives in West Sussex.

@EveAinsworth
www.eveainsworth.com